Amy Cross is the author of more than 200 horror, paranormal, fantasy and thriller novels.

OTHER TITLES
BY AMY CROSS INCLUDE

American Coven
Annie's Room
The Ash House
Asylum
B&B
The Bride of Ashbyrn House
The Cemetery Ghost
The Curse of the Langfords
The Devil, the Witch and the Whore
Devil's Briar
The Disappearance of Lonnie James
Eli's Town
The Farm
The Ghost of Molly Holt
The Ghosts of Lakeforth Hotel
The Girl Who Never Came Back
Haunted
The Haunting of Blackwych Grange
The Haunting of Nelson Street
The House on Fisher Street
The House Where She Died
Out There
Stephen
The Shades
The Soul Auction
Trill

THE HAUNTING OF MATTHEW THORNE

AMY CROSS

This edition
first published by Blackwych Books Ltd
United Kingdom, 2021

Copyright © 2021 Blackwych Books Ltd

All rights reserved. This book is a work of fiction.
Names, characters, places, incidents and businesses are
the product of the author's imagination or are
used fictitiously. Any resemblance to actual persons,
living or dead, or to actual events or locations,
is entirely coincidental.

Also available in e-book format.

www.blackwychbooks.com

CONTENTS

PROLOGUE
page 15

CHAPTER ONE
page 19

CHAPTER TWO
page 27

CHAPTER THREE
page 37

CHAPTER FOUR
page 45

CHAPTER FIVE
page 53

CHAPTER SIX
page 61

CHAPTER SEVEN
page 69

CHAPTER EIGHT
page 77

CHAPTER NINE
page 85

CHAPTER TEN
page 93

CHAPTER ELEVEN
page 101

CHAPTER TWELVE
page 109

CHAPTER THIRTEEN
page 117

CHAPTER FOURTEEN
page 125

CHAPTER FIFTEEN
page 133

CHAPTER SIXTEEN
page 141

CHAPTER SEVENTEEN
page 149

CHAPTER EIGHTEEN
page 157

CHAPTER NINETEEN
page 165

CHAPTER TWENTY
page 173

CHAPTER TWENTY-ONE
page 183

CHAPTER TWENTY-TWO
page 193

CHAPTER TWENTY-THREE
page 201

CHAPTER TWENTY-FOUR
page 209

CHAPTER TWENTY-FIVE
page 219

CHAPTER TWENTY-SIX
page 231

CHAPTER TWENTY-SEVEN
page 239

CHAPTER TWENTY-EIGHT
page 247

CHAPTER TWENTY-NINE
page 255

CHAPTER THIRTY
page 263

CHAPTER THIRTY-ONE
page 271

CHAPTER THIRTY-TWO
page 279

EPILOGUE
page 287

THE HAUNTING OF MATTHEW THORNE

PROLOGUE

SITTING ALONE IN THE gloomy hotel room, with the wet bikini still clinging to her body, Stella stared at the half-open door and waited for the sound to return.

In the distance, happy families were playing in the pool, splashing and laughing and yelling, but Stella had managed to ignore most of that noise and instead she was laser-focused on the door. She knew that the sound had been real, and that it had been moving steadily closer, and she also knew that there was no point running. After all, she'd tried running before, and how had that turned out?

A moment later she heard a scratching sound coming from the hallway, and she instantly tensed. She was on the verge of shivering, but not because of the cold fabric of her bikini. Instead, sheer terror had frozen her bones, and she knew only too well the face of the creature out in the hallway. The scraping sound was moving closer, and she knew that she'd finally run out of places to hide.

Suddenly she heard a faint gasp, and she instantly pulled back on the bed.

Somewhere outside, a child screamed, followed by a heavy splashing sound. The scream was nothing bad, just the squeal of a kid who was playing. More screams followed, while Stella sat in deathly silence and listened to the sound of the *thing* making its way along the corridor. She knew that at any moment, the old familiar face would appear and she'd see a pair of dead eyes staring back at her. She also knew, deep down, that she was too tired and scared to try running again.

"Please," she whispered, still watching the door, "just -"

Before she could finish, the scratching sound came to an abrupt halt. She felt a growing sense of nausea in the pit of her stomach, and she couldn't help but picture the awful sight that was waiting on the other side of the door. The effects of all the poolside alcohol had worn off; she was perfectly sober, and her heart was racing, and for the first time in many months she was once again having to remember to breathe.

Slowly, with a deep creaking sound, the door began to swing open.

Reaching down, Stella clutched the side of the bed as she waited for the inevitable sight. Had she ever really believed that she might escape? Perhaps at the start, at least when she'd managed to numb her fears with alcohol. Now, however, she knew that this moment had been coming for so very long. She'd never really had a chance of escaping.

The door swung open all the way. Outside, another child screamed.

CHAPTER ONE

Six months earlier...

BUZZING FRANTICALLY, SLOWLY TURNING in circles around the pin that had pierced its abdomen, the wasp tried desperately to get free.

"Look at the stupid little bastard," Gary said, squinting as he lifted his sunglasses and leaned closer to take a better look. "He's just going round and round."

Still the wasp tried to escape. The pin ran straight into its yellow-and-black striped body and held it stuck to a piece of rotten wood on the side of the pier leg. The buzzing sound was non-stop now and the wasp continually tried to fly away, as if it failed to understand how it was being held down.

"It's going to rip its belly open at this rate," Gary continued with a grin. "The poor bastard doesn't even realize that."

"Abdomen," Stella said.

"What?"

He turned to her.

"It's called the abdomen," she replied, lounging on the sand with a book propped against her knees, before turning to him. "That part of the insect, I mean. Their bodies have three parts.. There's the head, the thorax and the abdomen. We learned about it in school."

"Whatever."

"Can't you put it out of its misery?" she asked. "Why did you even do that to the poor thing, anyway?"

"Because I could," Gary told her. "Because it's a dumb bug and it doesn't know any better. It needs to learn who's above it on the food chain. Anyway, it was annoying me. It kept flying around and getting in my way. Stupid little bug."

He looked past her for a moment and watched tourists splashing in the sea, and he felt a shiver of disgust run through his bones. Nice was filled with tourists at the height of summer, and they crowded onto the beaches in such numbers that he sometimes wondered how they could all fit. His attention was briefly caught by a man wandering past, hawking cups of fruit along with various inflatables. Gary scrunched his nose for a couple of seconds, secure in the knowledge that no matter how bad things might get, he'd never be as lowly as some poor sod who made a living selling crap to holidaymakers.

"When did you suddenly give a damn, anyway?" he added, glancing at Stella again. "About bugs, I mean."

"Fine," she said with a sigh, turning to the next page of the book before giving up and setting it aside. "I swear, I'm roasting out here. I feel like all the water's just evaporating from my body. Can't we go somewhere else?"

"You don't like being on the beach now?"

"I think I'm going to dehydrate to death." She sat up on the sand. "Seriously, I'm tanned enough already."

"A little extra never hurt anyone," he suggested. "It's cheaper than using fake stuff, and you know all those rich guys love it." He reached over and put a hand on her knee. "Gotta keep thinking about the money. If you look at it a certain way, you're at work right now, getting that cute little body of yours into perfect condition."

"Can we go?" she asked. "Please? Just for

an hour or two."

"Go where?"

"I don't know," she said with another sigh, as heat from the midday sun continued to beat down and force sweat from her brow. "Anywhere."

Down on the rotten chunk of wood, the wasp was still pinned in place, twitching – and trying to escape from the burning sun – in its final moment of agony.

***

"We're going to work *that* place tonight," Gary said a few minutes later, as he and Stella walked along Nice's sun-soaked Promenade des Anglais, with the packed beach to their left. "Do you see that hotel over there? I guarantee you, the bar's going to be full of rich, drunk old guys who just want to forget about their saggy wives for a night."

"I don't like the look of it," she replied.

"Who cares about the look of it?" he asked, nudging her elbow. "They know your face in a lot of the other hotels, it's getting too risky. This place, on the other hand, is virgin territory."

They stopped and looked across the street, and they saw a doorman standing outside the hotel's grand entrance area.

"Maybe *virgin* isn't quite the right word," Gary added with a grin, "but you get the idea. It's a totally fresh hunting ground for you, and I've got a feeling you'll clean up. There's bound to be a bunch of silly old bastards in there who can afford to misplace their wallets. Then, once we've hoovered up a little more cash, we can get out of town and find somewhere fresh."

"But -"

"Nice is getting too risky," he said, interrupting her. "There's no way I can afford to pay those arseholes what I owe them, but they're a local outfit. In the grand scheme of things, they haven't got much reach. All we have to do is get a few kilometers out of town, and there's no way they'll be able to track us down. We'll be on someone else's turf."

"How much *do* you owe them?"

"You don't need to worry yourself about that."

"The drugs -"

"Will you just chill?" he asked, cutting her off again before putting an arm around her shoulder. "When have I ever let you down?"

"It's too warm," she replied, slipping free of his arm as she continued to watch the hotel. "I don't know, Gary, these really high-end hotels have much better security. You said it yourself, we're better off going for marks at the four-star places a little further along."

"That kind of talk's for quitters and losers," he told her. "I've got total faith in you, and I know you can hook a big fat fish or two." He looked down at the top of her shirt. "Just wear one of your sexiest outfits and make sure you've got plenty of skin on show."

She turned and glared at him.

"Why are you being like this?" he asked. "We've done this kind of thing loads of times before. This is our third summer in Nice."

"Last year, you told me we could stop doing this sort of thing."

"And we can."

He took hold of her by the sides of her arms, and this time he held tight as she tried to pull away.

"We just need a little more money," he continued, looking deep into her eyes even as she tried again to twist free. "Don't you remember the dream? Don't you remember what I told you a few years ago, when we were sitting in that bus shelter on a rainy afternoon in Dover?"

He waited.

"You *do* remember, right?" he added.

"Yes, but -"

"What did I tell you?"

"That if I stick with you, you'll make sure everthing's okay." She looked up at him, and now there was a hint of tears in her eyes. "I just thought that we'd survive by doing something less... illegal."

"You know I love you, right?"

She sighed.

"Tell me you know that, Stella."

"Of course I do."

"And you love me back, don't you?"

"Yes."

"Everything I do, I do for you," he added, before tapping her nose with the end of one finger. "Every damn thing. You're my reason for living, and I won't ever let you down. I just need you to work with me here, and rip off a few easy marks, and let me worry about the bigger picture. Besides, the guys in those bars, they don't *really* suffer. So they might lose a few hundred euros from their wallets, but so what? They can afford it. Most of them won't even notice it's gone. This is a victimless crime."

"The police wouldn't agree."

"The police don't give a damn, and neither should we," he replied, before forcing a smile. "One day, we're going to have our own little flat by the sea, and it'll be just you and me, and we'll look back on this time in our lives and we'll laugh."

"Do you promise?" she asked, even as she worried that she was being tricked. "That we won't be doing stuff like this forever, I mean. You said it'd just be while we get on our feet, but -"

"We'll be honest, upstanding members of society," he said firmly. "Everyone grifts a bit when they're younger. It's how the world's set up. Would you rather be working in some factory in Dover right now?"

She paused.

"No," she admitted finally.

"Then focus on the positives," he added, turning her around so that she was once again looking at the front of the hotel. "Focus on the fact that we're basically like Robin Hood. We take money from those who can afford to lose it. And who knows? Maybe, just maybe, tonight'll be our lucky night." He kissed the side of her face, as she watched the hotel with a growing sense of concern. "Maybe this'll be the night you meet a white whale and make enough money to set us up for life."

CHAPTER TWO

ALTHOUGH THE GRAND PIANO in the corner stood untouched, with a fine layer of dust indicating that it hadn't been played for some time, piano music nevertheless drifted across the hotel bar as diners clinked glasses and chatted over their meals.

Sitting alone at the bar, wearing a little black dress that showed plenty of cleavage, Stella took another small sip from her drink. She'd only budgeted for one cocktail per hour, but so far she'd been left entirely alone and she was starting to feel as if the evening was going to be a bust. She glanced at the clock on the far wall and saw that there were still a few minutes to go until eight o'clock rolled around, and then she looked over at the diners again and realized that they were all couples.

So far, she hadn't seen a single sad, lonely, potentially foolish old man.

A moment later, spotting movement by the door, she turned and saw a handsome middle-aged man stepping into the room. Her interest was instantly piqued as she realized that he seemed to be alone, and then she watched as the head waiter hurried over to attend to the man; this, she knew, meant that the new guest was important, and she instinctively sat up a little better and averted her gaze, hoping that the man might spot her at the bar. She knew that it would be a mistake to seem desperate, but she was very good at keeping track of things through the corner of her eye; looking down at her drink, she was still able to see that the head waiter was leading the man toward the far end of the room.

Finally she allowed herself to look again, and she was surprised to see that the man was being seated at a table in a booth, a little way from the rest of the diners. Clearly, then, her earlier assessment had been correct. This man was wealthy, or important, or most likely both.

"Hey," she said, turning to the bartender as he grabbed a couple of glasses from the shelf nearby, "do you know who that is over there?"

The bartender turned to her with a skeptical expression on his face, and then he looked toward the booth.

"Come on, you can tell me," Stella continued. "What's his deal?"

"Leave it," the bartender said in broken English.

"I'm just asking."

"Just leave it."

He turned to walk away.

"Is he royalty or something?" she asked. "I just want to know what he is."

"I don't know what he is," the bartender replied as he started mixing a drink, although after a moment he glanced at her. "I know what *you* are, though, and you're very close to being asked to leave the establishment."

"Is there any rule against a woman having a drink alone?" she asked, bristling at the loaded nature of his comment. She didn't know what she hated more: the fact that he was blatantly accusing her of being a prostitute, or the fact that he was right.

"I have drinks to make for people who have actual money to spend," he said, looking her up and down as if she was the filthiest specimen he'd ever seen in his life. "Don't cause trouble, okay?

Matthew Thorne isn't the kind of man who takes kindly to attention."

"Matthew Thorne?" she said with a smile. "Why, thank you so much for telling me his name."

As the bartender muttered something under his breath and walked away, Stella turned back to look at the booth. She watched as the man opened a menu, and already she was starting to fill with curiosity. She was accustomed to dealing with semi-rich visitors who wanted to splash some cash around, but something about Mr. Matthew Thorne seemed very different; he exuded wealth and confidence, as if even the fanciest hotel in all of Nice was somehow beneath him, and Stella couldn't deny that she was becoming more interested in him by the second.

And yet, for a moment, Stella felt as if the man wasn't alone. Although she couldn't see anyone sitting next to him, she couldn't shake the sense that a second gaze was staring back at her from the empty space to his left. She told herself that she had to be wrong, and after a few more seconds she was just about able to push such a strange idea out of her mind. She knew she couldn't afford to get jumpy.

Matthew Thorne was clearly off-limits, but finally – deciding that fortune might favor a bold move – she downed the last of her cocktail before getting up from the stool and starting to make her way across the room.

Suddenly a figure slammed into her from the right, almost knocking her off her feet. Startled, she turned and reached out, instinctively catching the stumbling man as he muttered a series of muffled expletives.

"Are you okay?" she asked.

"I'm fine!" he blustered, although as he took a step back she could immediately tell that he was on the wrong side of a bottle of wine. "I just tripped, that's all. This damn carpet's a death-trap!"

Looking down, Stella could see no step or loose scrap that might have caused the incident, but a moment later the man began to search through his pocket. In the process, he briefly pulled out a fat, bulging wallet stuffed with cash. He slipped the wallet away again, but Stella had already seen more than enough.

"I'm just trying to find the bathroom," the man said, clearly trying – but failing miserably – to appear sober. He was red-faced and puffy, and his eyes swam with alcohol. "You'd think they might have a few more signs out, but I suppose signs are too ordinary for a fancy place like this."

"I can show you the way," Stella said, quickly linking her arm with his and starting to lead him across the room. She knew an easy mark when she saw one, and she felt certain that he could be fleeced in the blink of an eye. "It'll only take a minute."

"Do you work here?" the man asked.

"Sort of," she replied with a smile.

She glanced at the bar and saw the bartender's disapproving stare, and then she looked over toward the booth. To her surprise, Matthew Thorne was staring straight at her with the most intense glare she'd ever seen in her life, but before she had a chance to smile she was already out in the corridor with the increasingly drunk, increasingly irritating man she'd rescued just a moment earlier.

***

"I swore I wouldn't drink too much tonight," the man groaned as he sat slumped on a toilet in a cubicle in the men's room. "I've got to be up so early in the morning."

"You'll be fine," Stella said, watching as he leaned over and rested his head against the cubicle's wall. "All you need is a little rest, and you'll be fit and fighting when the sun comes up."

"I don't have an alcohol problem," the man said, slurring his speech more than ever. His eyes were continually slipping shut, and his efforts to keep them open seemed to be faltering. "I can handle myself just fine, but when the cat's away, the cat likes to play. The other cat. You know what I mean."

He let out a sudden, very loud hiccup that shook his whole body.

"I'm a good boy, really," he continued, and now his eyes stayed shut. "If I have a fault, it's that I enjoy life a little too much. You know how it is, don't you? Life's for living, not for hiding away, but I suppose I just take that a tad too far at times." He sighed heavily. "Why must there be such a high price for enjoying oneself?" he added, before continuing with a series of mumbles that became less comprehensible by the second.

Finally his lips twitched a few times, as if he thought he was still talking, and then he nodded off.

Stella waited for a few seconds, but she already knew exactly what to do next. Working quickly and efficiently, she peeled the man's jacket open and reached into one of the pockets, and then she expertly slipped his wallet out before opening it up and seeing the huge collection of banknotes. She slipped the money out and quickly thumbed through it all, and she could already tell that she'd managed to get hold of at least a couple of thousand euros.

She slid the empty wallet back into the man's pocket, and then she got to her feet and took a few steps back.

"Sweet dreams," she whispered, before leaving the cubicle and making he way across the men's room.

As she opened the door, another man almost bumped straight into her.

"Little emergency," she told him, smiling as she saw the bemused expression on his face. "Nothing to get worked up about."

Once she was alone in the corridor, she took a moment to make sure that the money was safely stored away, and then she looked toward the door that led into the restaurant. Her usual policy was to split from a place as soon as she'd managed a decent score, but something about Matthew Thorne compelled her to head toward the door. She couldn't help thinking about the intensity of his stare, and she felt deep down that they'd definitely shared some kind of connection. No matter how hard she tried to persuade herself that she was making a mistake, she stopped in the doorway and looked over at the booth at the far end of the restaurant.

She felt an immediate sense of disappointment as she saw that Matthew Thorne was already gone. Evidently he hadn't even waited around to eat.

Trying to focus on the fact that she'd made a nice pile of money, Stella turned and headed out to the foyer. All she had to do now was take the cash home and add it to the nest-egg that she and Gary were going to use to buy a better future.

CHAPTER THREE

"SLOW DOWN!" SHE SNAPPED a couple of hours later, as she saw Gary handing another note over to the bartender at the little bar near the train station. "How much are you spending?"

"Chill," Gary replied, as he slid another mojito toward her. "A night like this calls for a proper celebration!"

"We're supposed to be saving this money!"

"We're going to save *almost* all of it," he said, rolling his eyes. "You made almost two and a half grand tonight. We can afford to splash out on a little party."

He leaned over and grabbed her by the arm, holding her a little too tight for comfort.

"What's the point of life if you don't have

fun now and again?" he added. "That's what we're here for, isn't it? That's the whole point of existing. We only get one go-round on this planet, so we have to make the most of it!"

"Are you buying drinks for your friends again?" she asked, glancing toward the tables on the far side of the room. "This is the third round you've got in, Gary. You can't just keep throwing our money away like this."

She waited for him to reply, but a moment later he leaned back over to the bartender and began to order some more drinks. In that instant, Stella realized with absolute certainty that the evening was going to follow the same tired pattern as usual, with Gary squandering their meager resources.

"Give me the money!" she said firmly.

He waved her away.

"Gary, I'm serious," she continued, grabbing his arm and trying to pull him back from the bar. "This money's supposed to be used for our future! How are we ever going to get out of this place if you keep drinking it all away? I earned that money and I want to look after it until we need it. Are you even listening to me?"

"Women, huh?" Gary said to the bartender. "Line them up, mate, okay?"

"So was it all a lie?" she asked, and now

there were tears in her eyes. "Were we never really going to leave Nice at all?"

"Of course we're going to leave Nice," he told her with a sigh, "just... I can't deal with this right now, okay? I'm trying to have a good time, and you're just nagging me to death."

"Fine," she replied, turning and storming out, straight past the table where Gary's friends were shouting and laughing. "Destroy our future. See if I care."

***

Sitting alone in an alley near the bar, with the sound of the party drifting through the cool night air, Stella sobbed gently and tried to stop herself screaming.

She knew she was stuck in an endless loop, that her life with Gary was just going round and round in circles without any hope of a future. The same thing happened every time: they talked about all their plans for the future, then they made a little money through some hare-brained and usually illegal scheme, and then they ended up frittering everything away so that they were right back where they started. The worst part, however, was the constant sense of hope, and the fact that Stella was always able to convince herself that this time things would be different.

"I hate you," she whispered through gritted teeth, thinking of Gary spending more and more of their cash. Deep down, however, she knew that those three words were a lie.

She didn't hate him.

She loved him.

"What's wrong with you?" she gasped, and now she was addressing herself. She knew she could go home to England at any moment, that she could stay with her mother and get a proper job and live a normal life.

All she had to do was dump Gary for good.

Taking a deep breath, she sniffed back more tears and tried to find the necessary bravery in her heart. She'd left Gary before, of course, but she'd always ended up taking him back. He had a way of finding her, of sneaking his way back into her affections, and she was starting to fear that she was never going to break free. At the same time, she worried that he wouldn't be able to survive on his own, and that she was the only person who was capable of keeping his life from falling apart. Sometimes she wondered whether what she felt for him was truly love, or whether it was actually a kind of intense pity.

After a few more seconds, suddenly feeling as if she was being watched, she looked along the alley and saw that a limousine was parked out on the street.

She waited, telling herself that limousines were hardly a rare sight in Nice, but she already felt as if somebody was staring at her from inside the vehicle. She found that she couldn't tear her gaze away and, as she continued to watch the limousine's dark window, she began to wonder why she could feel a tingling sensation on one side of her neck. Almost without thinking, she got to her feet and took a couple of steps forward, before reaching out to steady herself against the wall of the alley.

Matthew Thorne.

She had no idea why, but the image – the idea – of Matthew Thorne suddenly rushed into her mind with such force that she felt certain that he must be in the limousine. She knew that the odds of such a chance encounter were minuscule, of course, and that most likely she was letting her imagination run wild. Still, the more she stared at the limousine, the more certain she felt that it was *his* eyes that were watching her from behind the dark glass. Finally, stepping forward again, she realized that she was slowly being drawn to the vehicle as if by some invisible string.

Reaching the end of the alley, she told herself that she should go back into the bar and find Gary, but the sound of laughter and drinking seemed so far away now, as if they existed in another world. She swallowed hard, and she heard the sound of herself swallowing, and she took some more steps forward as she approached the side of the road. And then, as she looked at the limousine's door, she saw that it was very slowly starting to open.

"Stella!" a voice yelled suddenly.

Startled, she turned and saw Gary waving at her from the door to the bar. Feeling as if she'd woken from a dream, she stared at him for a moment before turning to the limousine, just in time to see that the door was now shut. A fraction of a second later, the limousine pulled away and joined the flow of traffic, quickly disappearing into the busy Nice night.

Unable to shake the sense that she'd made a terrible mistake, she continued to look along the street until she realized that somebody was approaching.

"Where did you get to?" Gary asked drunkenly, grabbing her arm for support. "Babe, let's not fight, yeah? You know I hate it when we fight, and there's really no point. You love me, and I love you, and we both love going with the guys to that nightclub round the corner, so why don't we just accept the inevitable?"

She turned to him.

"We're not going to a nightclub," she said firmly.

"Babe..."

"You can barely stand and -"

Before she could finish, she heard a heaving sound nearby, and she turned to see that Gary's friend Andy was throwing up just outside the bar. She winced, hating the fact that she was getting caught up in yet another of their drunken nights, but she knew there was already no way of backing out. The guys would have their hearts set on going to one of the many clubs in the area, and they wouldn't emerge until the sun was coming up again; she could head home and leave them to it, of course, but then she wouldn't be able to keep an eye on her boyfriend, and she knew from bitter experience that he could get into all sorts of trouble if he was left alone. A long night of babysitting lay ahead of her, even though her bones were aching and she desperately wanted to sleep.

"Babe?" Gary said, slurring his speech more than ever. "You're not going to be a drag, are you?"

"No, I'm not going to be a drag," she

replied, resigned to her fate now. "Just promise you won't keep buying drinks for them all night, okay? Let's try to keep at least some of the money I earned."

"That's the spirit!" he said, patting her hard on the back before turning and waving at the others. "Hey, over here! I got permission! We're going to party! The next round's on me!"

CHAPTER FOUR

"STEADY," STELLA SAID SEVERAL hours later, holding Gary carefully as she struggled to maneuver him down the alley that led to their flat. "How drunk *are* you?"

"I'm not drunk at all," he murmured, although he could barely get the words out. "You're just saying that because you always want to feel superior."

"You threw up five times on the walk back," she pointed out.

"That doesn't make me drunk. That makes me fun."

Stumbling, he reached out and supported himself against the wall.

Sighing, Stella waited to see whether he was going to throw up yet again. The flat was only a few yards away and she desperately wanted to get to bed, although she knew that first she'd have to deal with Gary's drunken attempts to prove that he was sober. There was a depressing routine to their big nights out and she figured it'd take at least an hour before he finally passed out on the sofa, most likely while trying to play some video game on the console he'd sworn he hadn't stolen.

"Nearly there," she muttered, resolving to just get him inside and worry about the rest later. "Come on."

Although Gary grunted a few comments under his breath, he managed – just about – to lean on her and follow her to the door. She, in turn, just about managed to get the key from her bag, and she was able to support Gary while she slipped the key into the lock. She could feel that he was on the verge of collapse, but she didn't mind that so long as he collapsed *inside* the flat. And then, as she began to turn the key, she realized to her horror that the door was already unlocked, which meant...

She froze for a moment, listening for any hint of an intruder. After a few seconds, with Gary increasingly melting against her, she pushed the door open. The hinges creaked, but the flat's dark interior showed no immediate signs of an intruder.

"Why aren't we inside yet?" Gary asked.

"Quiet!" she hissed, as she frantically thought back to the moment when they'd left the flat earlier.

She distinctly remembered locking the door. She was always very careful, especially in such a rough neighborhood; Gary mocked her constantly for double-checking and triple-checking everything, but she knew that it was important to be careful. There was no way she'd left the door unlocked.

She opened her mouth to call out, but at the last moment she stopped herself.

Suddenly Gary pushed past her and stumbled into the hallway. Before she could call him back, Stella watched as he slammed into the wall and lost his balance, and a second later she saw him crumpling down onto the floor with a loud groan.

"Will you be careful?" she snapped, stepping in after him and crouching down. Once she was sure he was okay, she looked along the hallway, but there was still no sign of anyone.

"Leave me here," Gary mumbled. "I'll be fine."

She was about to tell him that he had to at least get to the sofa, but in that instant she heard the telltale sound of that very same sofa creaking as somebody got to their feet in the living room. She realized instantly that the flat wasn't simply being burgled; that would be too easy, because there was a worse option that was already coming true. A moment later, hearing the soft slipping sound of footsteps, she took a deep breath before looking along the corridor again. This time, she saw a dark figure stepping into view.

"Don't worry about me," Gary groaned, rolling onto his back. "Leave me where I fell. I'll be absolutely dandy."

"Still looking after this infant, I see," a familiar voice said in the darkness.

Stella instantly flinched. She'd hoped to never hear that voice again, although deep down she'd known that the only way to escape was to leave Nice far behind. Sure enough, a moment later Walter stepped forward and she saw him staring down at her as Gary continued to let out a series of faint moans.

"Don't you ever get tired of hauling his sorry, drunk ass around town?" Walter asked with obvious contempt. "You're too good for him, Stella. He wouldn't last five minutes without you to constantly pick him up and hose him down. He'd have ended up floating face down in the harbor by now."

"What are you doing here?" she snapped, trying not to panic. "This is our flat, you have no right to break in!"

"You left the door open."

"No," she said firmly, "we didn't."

"Didn't you?" He shrugged. "My recollection must be a little faulty. Anyway, you have a nice place here. Some nice underwear in the drawers in the bedroom too. Then again, I guess it's easy to afford somewhere to live, when you're not in the habit of paying your debts."

"We don't owe you anything!"

"You might not, but your boyfriend here does."

Walter took another step forward.

"I think my boss has been a patient man," he continued, "but there comes a time when that patience starts to wear thin. Now, the way I see it, there are two options here. One, Gary's going to man up and find the money from somewhere, and do the honorable thing by paying off what he owes. Or, two, he's going to gather up just enough money to get out of town, and then he's going to hope that Cole's boys can't find him. The question is, which option is an idiot like Gary going to choose?"

"He doesn't owe anything!" Stella replied through gritted teeth. "He was set up!"

"He took some things that don't belong to him, and now he has to pay."

"You can't prove -"

"Consider this the last warning," Walter added, cutting her off. "After tonight, things are going to get a lot more forceful, if you catch my drift. Dear Gary has to pay off every cent he owes, and then he can walk away without a care in the world."

"He told me what happened," she said, slowly getting to her feet. "He told me it wasn't his fault that those drugs got lost. It was the couriers, they stole it all, and then they tried to blame Gary for the fact that nothing showed up in the lockers."

"Is that so?" Walter asked, raising a skeptical eyebrow. "And what about the gear Gary was seen selling a few weeks ago? If he didn't have anything to do with the vanishing shipment, then where *did* he get his supply from?"

"Gary wasn't selling drugs."

"Ask around and you'll soon find that I'm telling the truth," Walter told her with a faint smile. "The matter's not up for discussion. He owes fifty grand, and Cole's not going to wait a moment longer. When Gary sobers up, tell him that trying to skip town would be a really bad idea and that he needs to at least come up with a payment plan. He knows how to contact Cole, but he's running out of time." He looked down at Gary and chuckled. "If he's got the money to get this shit-faced, he should have the money to start paying his debt. That's only fair, don't you think?"

With that, he stepped past them both, heading toward the door.

"And what about Cole?" Stella asked. "What if someone blabbed his secrets all over town? It wouldn't go down well if the press found out that the son of one of the town's most respectable businessmen is involved in drugs."

"Are you threatening Cole?" Walter replied, stopping and turning to her.

"I'm just saying that this isn't one-sided," she said through gritted teeth. "Cole has a secret. He wouldn't want that to get out, would he?"

She waited, but Walter simply stared at her for a moment.

"Well?" she continued, and now her mouth was dry. "What if -"

"You think Cole has a secret?" Walter snapped, suddenly grabbing her by the throat and slamming her against the wall with such force that she let out a brief, involuntary cry. "Is that what you call it?" he sneered, leaning closer to her face. "A secret? No, little lady, that's not what it is at all. A secret is a game. A secret is something you keep, and think about exposing. It's something you maybe use to threaten people." He leaned even closer. "Cole doesn't have secrets. Cole simply has facts that aren't ever going to get out, and if you try to turn that into a game by calling it a 'secret', then you'll very quickly discover that there are limits to his generosity."

She opened her mouth to reply, but she quickly realized that her best bet was to simply stay quiet. Anything she said would only make matters worse.

"You and your wastrel of a boyfriend know

what needs to happen," Walter sneered, peppering her face with spit. "It's really that simple. Make arrangements to pay the money back, or suffer the consequences."

Letting go of her throat, he turned and walked away, leaving Stella to slide down the wall until she was sitting on the floor just a few feet from Gary. She looked up and saw Walter stepping out of the flat, and she breathed a sigh of relief as she realized that he was gone, at least for now.

"Gary?" she said, her voice trembling with fear. "Did you hear all that?"

She waited, and then – hearing a faint snoring sound – she turned to see that he was completely unconscious.

"Damn you!" she hissed.

Putting her head in her hands, she tried to think of some way out of the mess. Realizing that the situation was hopeless, however, she quickly broke into a series of desperate sobs.

CHAPTER FIVE

"DO YOU HAVE TO yell?" Gary groaned the next day, as he sat wearing dark glasses outside a bar near the beach. "My head's throbbing."

"I'm not yelling," Stella pointed out, unable to hide the sense of irritation in her voice. "And don't ask for any sympathy from me, because you did all of this to yourself."

She took a sip of water.

"I'm not just talking about the hangover, either," she added, before leaning toward him across the table. "That asshole was in our flat, Gary! You swore to me that they didn't know where we lived!"

"Can you give me a break?"

"Are we actually going to leave Nice?" she asked. "Can you be honest with me for once? Are we ever going to leave this town, or is that something you keep telling me to... string me along?"

She waited for an answer, but after a few seconds she realized that – behind his sunglasses – Gary was looking at something behind her. She hesitated for a moment longer, and then she turned to see a group of middle-aged women eating at a table near the exit. For a few seconds she couldn't work out why Gary might be interested in something so mundane, but then she saw that one of the women had left her handbag a little way from the table, right next to the door.

She turned to Gary again, and then she sighed.

"You've got to be kidding me," she told him.

"I just -"

"We come here a lot!" she said firmly. "Are you seriously going to steal that thing?"

"There are thousands of bars in Nice," he pointed out, still watching the bag. "You're the one who's so keen to leave town. It's a bit hypocritical of you to also get annoyed if we can't come back to one particular, scummy little bar."

"I can't believe you're actually contemplating doing this," she replied, rolling her eyes. "You're never going to pay Cole off by nicking a few bags here and there."

"It's a start, though," he said, getting to his feet. "You go out first. And once you're on the street, meet me at the usual spot."

***

"Stupid cow!" Gary snarled, as he tipped the rest of the bag's contents onto the pavement and then leaned back against the wall. "What kind of idiot goes out with just a few coins?"

"She had her purse on the table," Stella replied. "I told you that! Come on, was this really worth racing along the street like an idiot for?"

Hearing a police siren, she turned and looked over her shoulder. A moment later a police car flashed past the junction, and she breathed a sigh of relief as she realized that they weren't going to have to run again, at least not for now. At the same time, she couldn't shake the feeling that the world was closing in around them, as if something in the air was warning her that time was running out. She'd felt that way ever since the previous night.

"You're going to have to score big," Gary said.

She turned to him.

"I'm sorry," he continued, eyeing her with a fearful expression, "but if you don't manage to hook a few big prizes in the next week, we're in serious danger."

"What exactly do you expect me to do?" she

asked.

"What you do best." He fixed her with a determined stare, before reaching out and taking her hand. "I've got total faith in you, Stella. I know what you're capable of, all you have to do is conjure up some more confidence and really go for it. Take it up a notch. The guys in those hotels are wallowing in cash, they shed it like a dog sheds hair. The marks are out there, you've just got to connect with them."

"You think I can rustle up fifty thousand like that?" she said, unable to believe what she was hearing. "In a week?"

"I'll go to Cole and negotiate a deal," he told her. "I can do that. He'll listen to me, he'll cut what we owe by half or... whatever. But then we really have to deliver."

"*I* really have to deliver, you mean," she replied. "And let's be honest here, you're the one who owes the money. Doesn't it seem unfair to you that you're getting me to do this?"

"Do you want out?" he asked, before reaching over and touching the side of her face. "I'd understand if you did. If you want to walk away right now, I won't hold it against you. You can go back to England and live a normal life, you can do all the normal things that people do. I won't hate you for that, Stella. In fact, I'd almost envy you. There's really no need for you to stick around and support me, not when I'm such a screw-up."

He ran a finger across her cheek, as if to wipe away an imaginary tear.

She opened her mouth to reply, and then she sighed. For a fraction of a second, she allowed herself to imagine all the fear lifting from her shoulders. Almost immediately, however, she knew that her heart would break if she left Gary behind.

"I love you," she told him, with tears in her eyes. "You know that. I just wish we could live an easier life, that's all."

"And we will," he replied with a faint smile, "just as soon as we find a new place to live. Somewhere far from here, somewhere we can start over. No-one'll know us, we'll just be a pair of idiots in love who settle down and start thinking about having a family of our own. You want that, don't you?"

She paused, and then she nodded.

"More than anything," she whispered.

"I'll give you all of that and more," he added. "A million times over. All you have to do is stick with me."

"So I'm going to hit the hotels big," she replied, sniffing back the first hint of tears. "The top hotels, the really posh ones, and I'm going to do several each night. No more slacking, no more resting on my laurels. Tonight I'm going to do those three down on the strip, and then maybe a couple up toward the big gardens. At this time of year, there have to be lots of guests there who are just ripe for the picking." She took a deep breath. "It'll be one last big push to get the money we need."

"That's the spirit," he said with an eager grin. "I knew I could count on you."

"I can do this," she said, before sighing heavily. "I know I can, and it'll be easier if I know that it's the last time. I'll just shut my mind off and forget who I really am, and by the end of the week I'll have made all the money we're ever going to need. I just need to -"

"Think of the great life we're going to have," Gary said, interrupting her. "Sun, sea, sand, booze, nothing but fun and games forever. All my old mates from school are working in factories or offices back in England, or cleaning the streets or slogging through shifts in pubs. That's not living, it's surviving, but we're better than that. We're too smart to get caught up in that sort of thing." He nudged her elbow. "That's what I've always loved about you, Stella. You see the world that way I do. You know there's no point settling for a boring life."

"We *could* go back," she said tentatively. "We could get proper jobs and -"

"No!" he said firmly, putting his hands on the sides of her head and holding her firmly. "Don't ever think like that. Don't weaken. Our future's out here in the sun. We're so close, let's not give up now. Think about your dad and what happened to him."

"I -"

"What happened to him, Stella?"

"He worked his ass off every day until he was in his sixties," she said cautiously, "and then he dropped dead of a heart attack just as he was due to retire. He knew there was a heart condition that runs in our family, but he never thought it'd get him like that."

"He played it by the book, and he never got any kind of reward. Babe, he'd be proud of you. He'd recognize that you're living your own life, in your own way."

She hesitated. Deep down, she liked the idea of a safe, boring job in an office somewhere, living without constant fear. She knew she couldn't admit that to Gary, however, so she told herself that she had to keep faith in their plans. She'd already sacrificed so much in order to be with him, and she figured there was no way she could give up when they were so close to their dream.

Suddenly, hearing a siren coming closer, she looked along the street and saw a police car turning the corner.

"Move!" Gary hissed, grabbing her by the hand and jumping to his feet, then leading her away from the cafe.

"But -"

"It's probably not for us," he continued, his voice filled with tension, "but I don't want to take the risk. There's no need to -"

Before he could finish, the siren changed its tone and they both heard the car racing toward them.

"Run!" Gary yelled, leading her down an alley. "Move it! Don't let them see your face!"

CHAPTER SIX

"ARE YOU GOING TO drink that cocktail or just stare at it all night?"

Startled, Stella looked up and saw that the barman was watching her. She was in a new hotel near the old part of town, sitting all alone at the bar in the hope that somebody would approach, and she was more than accustomed to the way hotel workers tended to have her pegged from the outset. Still, that didn't make their dirty looks feel any less stinging, and she immediately felt her resolve strengthen.

"Is there a time limit?" she asked.

"I just thought it can't be much fun, sitting there like that," the barman said sniffily. "Not unless..."

His voice trailed off.

"Are you always rude to customers?" she

asked.

"*Are* you a customer?" he replied. "Or are you the one who's selling something tonight?"

Realizing that she didn't have the time or the energy to engage in conversation, Stella turned and looked across the room. Once again, she saw lots of couples but precious few single men, and she was starting to wonder when her seam of bad luck was going to end. Even as she peered at the individual tables and hoped for some sign of a chance, she couldn't help but notice that she was once again being ignored. Sometimes she wondered whether word had spread, and whether everyone had been shown her photo and told not to even look at her, but she told herself that she was being paranoid; she needed the money, and there had to be some potential marks somewhere.

And then she saw him.

Spotting movement at the far end of the room, she was surprised to see Matthew Thorne entering the room. Once again he was alone, and once again he was being shown to a table by the head of the house. Unable to tear her gaze away, Stella watched as he walked slowly and calmly between the other tables like a lion stalking his prey. Something about Matthew Thorne struck her as being hopelessly powerful, and she could tell that the energy in the room had changed. The other guests seemed determined to not look at Thorne, although one or two of the men cast fearful glances in his direction once he'd made his way past. Although she had no idea who he was or why he commanded such respect, Stella could tell one thing for certain: Matthew Thorne was at the top of the social food chain, at least in the bars and restaurants of Nice.

She watched him take his seat, and then she forced herself to keep looking at him as he took a menu from the waiter. Willing him to return her gaze, she watched him intently, until finally he glanced in her direction and their eyes met.

Again, however, she felt as if somebody else was watching her. She looked at the space either side of Matthew Thorne and saw no sign of anyone, yet the feeling persisted as she felt another pair of eyes burning into her soul. Part of her wanted to get up and hurry out of the room, but she told herself that she had to stay firm and that – besides – Matthew Thorne might be a real jackpot. She couldn't afford to look too desperate, of course, so after a few seconds she looked at him again, allowed herself a faint smile, and then turned back to her drink.

Was he still watching?

Was he making his way over?

Resisting the urge to look at him again, she focused on her drink and tried to calm her mind. Thorne had been staring at her, that much was certain, but she wasn't sure that she'd managed to hook him just yet. Telling herself to remain calm, and that she still had a little time, she finished her cocktail and then looked over at the bartender. To her surprise, she saw that he was already on his way to her with another drink.

"From the gentleman over there," he said, clearly unimpressed, as he set the glass down in front of her.

Glancing over her shoulder, Stella saw to her surprise that Matthew Thorne was focusing on the menu. A moment later, however, she spotted a different man waving at her from a table in the corner. She felt a flutter of irritation that he, not Thorne, was her admirer, but she quickly realized that the man looked like a decent mark. She paused for a few seconds, before taking a sip from her drink and then getting to her feet.

***

"Are you sure you don't want to join me?" Harold called out from the bathroom, as the shower continued to run. "It's getting nice and soapy in here, and there's more than enough room!"

"In a moment," she replied, trying to sound relaxed as she frantically searched through the jacket on the chair. "Make sure it's really steamy for me!"

As soon as she found his wallet, she began to check for cash. Finding none, she instead pulled out a few credit cards; she knew Gary would be able to work his magic, so she quickly shoved those into her pocket before slipping the wallet back into place. She checked the rest of the pockets, convinced that a guy like Harold would have some rolls of notes somewhere, and then she got to her feet.

At that moment, Harold began to sing loudly in the shower.

"Asshole," Stella muttered under her breath, as she realized that she'd endured Harold's grubby hands all over her body for almost an hour, with almost nothing to show for her work. She'd pegged him as the kind of rich, slightly dithering older guy who'd lose track of cash in his hotel room, but she realized now that he wasn't going to offer a great payday after all.

She listened for a moment to make sure that he was still busy in the bathroom, and then she hurried to the door and pulled it open.

"I know for a fact that you're a dirty girl right now," he called to her. "Why don't let me wash off some of that -"

As soon as she'd bumped the door shut, Stella set off along the corridor, quickening her pace with each step as she made for the elevator at the far end. Although she was fairly sure that Harold wouldn't notice her absence for another couple of minutes, she was determined to get out of the hotel and reach her next target. Sex with Harold had been an uncomfortable, dispiriting experience that she wanted to forget already, and she felt sick to her core as she realized what she'd become. She wanted to blame Gary, but deep down she knew that only one person was responsible for her decisions.

"Come on," she muttered under her breath as she jabbed at the button on the panel next to the elevator's door. "What's taking so long?"

After glancing over her shoulder, she turned and headed to the fire escape. She knew that there were lots of cameras in the hotel, and that she couldn't rely on a guy like Harold showing some discretion. Most men would never want to admit that they'd been robbed by someone they'd met in a bar, especially when money had changed hands, but she knew that occasionally an idiot might decide to make a fuss. As she hurried down the stairwell, she stopped for a moment to remove her heels before setting off again, and by the time she got to the bottom she was out of breath.

Pushing the door open, she rushed into the foyer and hurried toward the door.

"M'am?"

Stopping suddenly, she spun around and saw that a man from the reception desk was standing just a few feet away.

"M'am," he continued, holding a piece of paper out toward her, "I believe this is for you."

Frozen in fear for a moment, Stella couldn't quite summon the strength to respond. She was terrified that Harold might have called down from his room and demanded to get the police involved, but after a few seconds she realized that most likely she was overreacting. Still, she was struggling to keep from showing her fear, and all she wanted to do was get as far away from the hotel as possible.

"M'am?" the man said cautiously. "Are you alright?"

"I'm fine," she blurted out, before taking the piece of paper. "Why? What's it got to do with you?"

"Enjoy the rest of your evening, M'am," the man replied superciliously, before turning and walking away.

Glancing around, Stella saw no sign of anybody else watching her, so she hurried out of the hotel. As soon as she was on the street, she stopped and took a look at the piece of paper. She felt her heart miss a beat as she saw that the note was written on a piece of paper with Matthew Thorne's name and phone number embossed at the top, and with a simple message written underneath in neat handwriting:

Call me.

CHAPTER SEVEN

"WHAT'S GOT YOU IN such a mood tonight?" Gary muttered testily as he continued to count the money Stella had made during the evening. "Anyone'd think you don't love your job."

"Just tell me how much there is."

He finished with the final stack of notes, before leaning back in the plastic chair and sighing.

"Eight hundred," he said with a heavy sigh. "Babe, that's a good effort, but we're never going to get out of trouble at this rate."

"I can do better."

"It might be time to consider -"

"I said, I can do better!" she snapped, before realizing that she was letting her frustration take control. Getting to her feet, she hurried across the front room and stopped at the window. She moved the curtain aside and looked out at the alley, watching for any sign that Walter or some other goon might already be back.

"So what happened tonight?" Gary asked. "Were there just not many marks about or..."

His voice trailed off, and he let the question linger in the air for a few seconds.

"You've been out of sorts since you got back," he told her. "I've never seen you like this before, it's like you're really rattled. You understand why I'm worried, right? You usually laugh everything off, but you're not acting like yourself."

Again he waited for her to reply.

"Everyone has a bad night now and again," he continued finally, "and eight hundred's not to be sniffed at. In normal circumstances, I'd be happy. It's just that these aren't normal circumstances. We're still in a whole heap of trouble when Cole's guys come back."

Stella watched the alley for a moment longer, but deep down she knew that she was really trying to distract herself. She could feel Matthew Thorne's folded note in her pocket, as if it had a weight and a presence all of its own, and she couldn't shake the feeling that sooner or later she was going to have to look at it again. She'd considered throwing it away during the walk home, but she couldn't quite understand *why* she'd felt that way; after all, the note was just a note, just a piece of paper, so why did she feel as if her soul was vibrating?

"Babe?"

"What?" she asked, turning to him and immediately seeing the puzzled look on her face.

"Did something happen?" he said cautiously, before standing and making his way over to her. "Did someone hurt you, or scare you? Babe, if anyone laid a finger on you, give me his name and I swear I'll track the bastard down and -"

"No-one hurt me," she said firmly.

"Then what's got you all worked up?"

She paused, before realizing that she really had no choice other than to explain. Reaching into her pocket, she pulled out the piece of paper and handed it over.

"What's this?" Gary asked as he unfolded the note. He read the message. "Who's Matthew Thorne?"

"This guy at the hotel."

"What kind of guy at the hotel?"

"A rich guy. I don't know, I didn't talk to him."

"But he gave you this note?"

"He had someone give it to me. An employee at the hotel."

"And why would he do that if he's never met you?"

"I don't know!" she hissed, before sighing

again. "I suppose I caught his eye, not just tonight but last night as well. He was there, he was eating alone, or at least I think he was alone."

"You *think*?"

She thought back to the darkness that had seemed to surround Matthew Thorne both times.

"It's nothing," she stammered. "Can we please just drop it?"

"You didn't mention him before."

"That's because there was nothing to mention!" she pointed out, once again unable to hide her sense of exasperation. "I don't know why he gave me this note, okay? I caught him watching me a couple of times."

"Why didn't you go over and introduce yourself?"

"I don't know."

"It sounds like he's gagging for it," he continued. "This could be the answer to our prayers. If this guy's really into you, and it seems like he is, then he might be willing to pay big bucks for a fun night. Some of these guys are so loaded, they don't even know how much money they're spending, it's like confetti to them. Which hotel's he staying at?"

"I don't know."

"You need to try to be more -"

"There's something about him," she added, cutting him off. "I can't explain it, but both times I saw him, I felt as if something was... wrong, somehow."

"Wrong in what way?"

"I don't know."

He paused, before looking down at the note again.

"Your problem," he told her, "is that you overthink things. That's what you're doing right now, and there's really no need. This situation's pretty damn simple, Stella. You know exactly what you need to do."

"And what's that?"

He looked at her, before holding the note up so that she could once again see those two handwritten words:

Call me.

***

"You've reached the private office of Matthew Thorne," a man's voice said on the other end of the line. "How can I be of assistance?"

With a heavy sense of anticipation weighing in her chest, Stella briefly considered cutting the call. She was standing in the kitchen and she could feel her heart pounding; she had no idea why she was so nervous, but it was as if the universe was warning her to stop. She'd not even expected anyone to answer at such a late hour, but Gary had insisted that she should at least try.

"Hello?" the man continued. "Is anybody there?"

"Say something!" Gary hissed from the doorway.

"My name's Stella Ward," Stella said, trying to hide the fear in her voice. "I was... I mean, I got a note and..."

She took a deep breath as she realized that she had no way to explain the situation.

"Ms. Ward," the man replied, "yes, I was advised to expect a telephone call from you. Am I to understand that you wish to take Mr. Thorne up on his offer?"

"Offer?"

She glanced over at Gary and saw the expectant grin on his face. All she wanted to do was end the call and forget about Matthew Thorne entirely, but she knew that wasn't an option.

"What offer?" she asked cautiously.

"Mr. Thorne would like to invite you to dinner," the man explained. "It's rather late now and I imagine Mr. Thorne will already have eaten, so shall we arrange a time for tomorrow evening? Perhaps seven o'clock?"

"He wants to have dinner with me?" she replied, as Gary gave her a thumbs up. "Why?"

"I'm afraid Mr. Thorne didn't go into detail when he told me to expect your call," the man replied calmly, "only that he's keen to speak to you at the earliest available opportunity. Are you free tomorrow evening, or do we need to find another time?"

"Well, I..."

She hesitated, before looking over at Gary and seeing there was no way she could delay things.

"I'm free tomorrow evening," she said cautiously, "but -"

"Then it's settled," the man told her. "Dinner will be served promptly at seven and Mr. Thorne is a stickler for punctuality, so might I suggest that he has a car pick you up at five? If you'd like to give me your address, I'll arrange for -"

"No!" she blurted out suddenly, before she could stop herself. "I mean, I'd rather be picked up from a hotel. Is that okay?"

"How about the Millenianno?" the man suggested. "If you wait in the foyer, the driver will arrive for you at precisely five o'clock tomorrow evening I *would* ask, Ms. Ward, that you're on time."

Stella opened her mouth to reply, but the words stuck in her throat. Although the situation seemed harmless enough so far, and despite Gary's obvious enthusiasm, she couldn't shake the feeling that all the shadows of the world were turning and starting to close in around her. She knew she was taking too long to answer, but a growing sense of nausea was crawling its way up her chest and she realized after a few seconds that she couldn't possibly agree to meet Matthew Thorne for dinner. Somehow she knew that if she met him for even one moment, something awful would happen. The more she tried to ignore that sensation, the more she felt as if she was about to scream.

"She'll be there," Gary said suddenly, leaning into the phone and then tapping to end the call. "Right," he continued, patting her hard on the back, "we've got a little under twenty-four hours to get you all dolled up and looking the part. I think this might even call for a new dress!"

CHAPTER EIGHT

"DARLING, LET'S GO! WE don't want to be late meeting Charles and Terja!"

As she sat in the foyer of one of Nice's grandest hotels, wearing a revealing black dress that Gary had picked out for her, Stella looked over her shoulder and saw a young couple stepping out from one of the elevators. Glamorous and rich, and clearly carefree, they walked with interlinked arms toward the main door.

"Do we really have to go to dinner with those two tonight?" the man asked. "I'd much rather it was just you and me."

"You'll be fine," the woman replied, stopping and turning to adjust his tie. "You know you always enjoy it when you get there. You and Charles will be talking about business in no time."

"Fine," he replied with a smile, before leading her outside, "but tomorrow I get you all to myself. I'm taking you out and spoiling you."

"You'd better!"

Stella watched as the couple hurried to a waiting taxi. She could tell that they were completely in love, and she couldn't help but wonder what it must be like to live a life that was so easy. She knew she was probably misjudging the situation, and that everyone had pressures and stresses beneath the surface, but she still couldn't help feeling as if she and Gary spent every waking second trying to ignore the fact that their lives were falling apart. Some people, on the other hand, seemed to move effortlessly through life in a state of eternal bliss and happiness.

"Good evening, M'am," the man from the counter said as he walked past with a grin on his face. "Back again, I see."

She managed a half smile, before looking down and adjusting the cleavage of her dress. She'd told Gary that she was revealing too much flesh, that a man like Matthew Thorne would want to use his imagination. Gary had initially wanted to buy a dress that was about two sizes too small, but she'd talked him into something a little more respectable, although she was having to adjust herself every few minutes to make sure that she didn't come spilling out. She felt deeply uncomfortable, and she couldn't help but worry that this would start to show in her demeanor.

"Ms. Ward?"

Startled, she looked up and saw that a man was standing just a few feet away. Immediately getting to her feet, she could already tell that he was a driver, and sure enough she saw that the clock on the wall showed the time as precisely five o'clock. So far, everything seemed to be going according to plan.

"This way," the driver continued, gesturing toward the door. "I have the car waiting right outside."

***

As the limousine wound its way along a dark, meandering road outside the town, Stella felt her phone buzz yet again. Looking down, she couldn't ignore a flicker of irritation as she saw another message from Gary:

Are you there yet? What's it like?

She glanced at the driver and saw that he seemed to be focusing very much on the road, and then she quickly typed a reply:

Not yet. I told you to stop texting me.

Instantly, she saw that he was typing again, and she couldn't help imagining him frantically tapping at his phone as he sat lurking in their tight little flat.

"Come on," she whispered under her breath, "give me a break."

What's his house like?

She typed a reply:

How would I know? I'm not there yet!!!

He started typing again:

Call me when you get there, and then leave the line open. I want to hear everything that happens.

She quickly replied:

No way!!!

The response was almost instant:

I want to make sure you're safe! You're going to some random dude's house, you normally just do hotels! I want to make sure he doesn't start battering you about!

She thought for a moment, and then she spotted a light ahead. Sure enough, the car slowed a little as a set of gates began to swing open. Realizing that she must be getting close to her destination, she typed out another message:

I'm turning my phone off. I'll call when I'm done. Trust me, I'll be fine.

She quickly deleted those last five words and sent the message. Immediately, she saw that he was already typing another reply, but she quickly pressed the button on the phone's side, switching it off completely. Although she still felt a strong sense of dread in her chest, she figured that it was too late to back out of the meeting now, and the last thing she wanted was to have Gary eavesdropping on the whole thing. She told herself that it was his fault she was in such a mess in the first place, in which case there was no harm in letting him stew a little. Besides, she had no reason to worry that Matthew Thorne might be dangerous.

A few seconds later the car came to a halt, although the light in the distance was still a fair way off.

"We've arrived at Mr. Thorne's estate," the driver announced. "I'm afraid you'll have to complete the final stretch of the journey on foot."

Climbing out of the car, he made his way around and opened the door.

"This is an unfortunate necessity," he continued as he stepped aside and gestured for Stella to climb out. "Mr. Thorne has his ways."

Stella hesitated for a moment, before grabbing her purse from the seat and then stepping out of the car. The air was noticeably cooler now that she was up in the hills beyond Nice, although she could just about make out the glittering lights of the city far below. Turning, she looked along the driveway and spotted the lights of a grand house a couple of hundred meters away. At that moment, a breeze blew past and pushed a couple of stands of hair across her face, which she quickly had to put back in place.

She turned to the driver.

"Mr. Thorne will be waiting for you," he explained, with just a hint of unease in his voice. "I've already informed him that you're here."

"You have?"

She paused.

"I didn't hear you call him," she added.

"Please, don't waste any more time here with me," he replied, as he shut the car door. "I shall see you again when you leave. I'm sure you'll have a very pleasant time with Mr. Thorne. I hear that he's an extremely generous host and... Well, he was in the past, at least."

"In the past?"

"Good evening, Ms. Ward."

With that, he made a point of turning his back to her as he climbed back into the car, and Stella realized that she wasn't going to get any more information from him. As the limousine's engine started again and the vehicle turned around, she stood aside, and in that moment she noticed that the car certainly looked like the one that had been parked in the street a couple of days earlier, when she'd felt as if she was being watched. Then again, she quickly told herself that one black limousine looked pretty much the same as any other, and that she shouldn't get too carried away.

She waited until the vehicle's tail lights disappeared into the distance, and then she watched as the large iron gates began to whir shut. She briefly considered rushing forward and slipping back out through the gap while there was still a chance, but she waited too long and the gates finally bumped shut with a faint clanging sound.

Taking a deep breath, clutching her purse, Stella turned and looked toward the house. She still worried that she was getting into something dangerous, but she knew she had no choice. Even as she began to make her way along the driveway, she felt as if she wasn't entirely in control, as if external forces – Gary, and Matthew Thorne, and the people at the hotel – had somehow conspired to shape what happened to her. She was on rails, forced to do as fate decreed, and she felt a growing sense of resignation as she looked up at the facade of the house and noticed that not only was it huge, but it was also mostly dark.

Only a few downstairs lights were on as she reached the end of the driveway and looked at the large set of steps that led up to the front door.

She swallowed hard, just as the door opened and a figure stepped out. With the light from inside the house behind him, the figure was bathed in shadows as he stopped at the top of the steps, but from his outline alone Stella could already tell that this was Matthew Thorne himself.

"Good evening, Ms. Ward," he said darkly, as a shiver ran through her bones. "I've been expecting you."

CHAPTER NINE

"I DON'T KNOW WHETHER Jerome told you," Matthew said as he led Stella into the mansion's magnificent hallway, "but my staff are not allowed onto the property after nightfall. Once the sun has gone down, I prefer that they stay well away."

Stopping beneath the grand chandelier that hung down from a high ceiling, he turned to her, allowing her to see his handsome features for the first time that night. In the flickering light of the candles that burned on a table nearby, his cheekbones seemed more angular than ever, and the darkness of his eyes stared back at her with such intensity that she had to force herself to not turn away. For a few seconds, Matthew Thorne pinned her in place with a gaze that left her unable to move, unable even to breathe.

"Are you alright, Ms. Ward?" he asked cautiously. "You seem a little... stiff."

Taking a deep breath, she forced a smile that she immediately knew was askew and a mistake.

"I think I'm just overawed by your beautiful home," she told him, making a show of looking around. As she did so, she saw various doors leading off the hallway, and more at the top of the stairs, and she was suddenly struck by the sadness of such a large house standing so empty. "It's really nice up here."

"The house itself is from the early nineteenth century," Matthew explained, "and I've made no material alterations in the decade that it's been in my care. I don't really think of myself as owning the house, you see. It's more a case of me being lucky enough to be its custodian for now, just the... latest in a long line of people who have looked after the place and tried to keep it from falling into disrepair."

Turning to him, she wasn't quite sure how she was supposed to respond.

"Where are my manners?" he continued. "Please, will you come through and take a drink with me? Dinner has been left by my chef and will be ready at seven, but first I should like to... get to know you a little better. This way, please."

He turned and walked through a set of double doors, leaving Stella to take another deep breath. She wasn't sure how, or why, but something strange had happened when she'd first entered the house: for the first time in her life, she was having to remember to breathe, to take every single breath; something that had always been so natural now required focus and attention, and she worried that if she forgot, she might immediately begin to suffocate.

***

"I believe this used to be the library when the house was first built," Matthew explained a few minutes later, as he finished pouring two glasses of wine. "I'm afraid I don't have enough books to fill the place, so my library is a rather barren little corner in the office, which in turn means that this room stands empty a lot of the time. I really only use it when I'm entertaining."

Watching him carefully, still trying to work out his reasons for inviting her, Stella couldn't help but notice that his hands were shaking slightly as he set the decanter down. The shaking stopped, however, as he picked up the two glasses and carried them over to her.

"Which isn't very often," he added, with a hint of sadness in his voice. "Please, this is a wonderful red from 1979, one of the best years for this particular vineyard. I've been saving the bottle for... well, for a special occasion."

Stella hesitated, before realizing that she was supposed to take the glass.

"I'm so very glad you could make it tonight," Matthew told her. "I know you must have had your doubts, and probably some concerns as well. I can assure you that you're completely safe here, and that I am a gentleman. As you might have picked up from my accent, I – like you – was born in the United Kingdom. My family is from Cornwall, actually, although I doubt you would have noticed any of *that* heritage in my voice." He paused, and then he smiled. "Forgive me, I'm talking about myself far too much. A toast, to new beginnings."

"New beginnings," she repeated, somewhat puzzled, before taking a sip of wine.

"I told you it was a good year," Matthew continued once he'd taken a sip of his own. "Cases of this stuff are increasingly rare, one has to know which strings to pull in order to get any bottles at all. Fortunately I stashed some away many years ago, back when I first case here, so I don't have to worry too much. For now, at least."

"It's nice wine," she agreed, although she felt a little foolish for not being able to add anything more sophisticated. She'd drunk plenty of wine over the years, but she'd never picked up much in the way of wine knowledge. "Great... terroir," she added, using a word she'd heard a few times. "It really picks up the -"

Suddenly spotting movement out of the corner of her eye, she turned and looked at the door. She was sure she'd seen somebody standing there, but now there was no sign of anyone.

"Are you alright, Ms. Ward?" Matthew asked, not for the first time.

"Is there someone else here with us?" she replied, keeping her eyes fixed on the door.

Matthew turned and followed her gaze, before looking back at her.

"I'm sorry," Stella continued, realizing that she could hear nothing but silence. "I think it was just a trick of the light, something like that."

"Did you see someone?" he asked.

She opened her mouth to reply, and then she hesitated for a moment.

"No," she said, not wanting to seem foolish. She was more aware than ever of her lungs, and of the fact that her body needed her to keep breathing in and breathing out. The process was no longer automatic. "Do you really live up here all by yourself? That must get lonely, especially at night."

"As you are no doubt aware," he replied, "I often go out in the evenings. To local hotels, restaurants, that sort of thing."

"Which is where you saw me," she pointed out.

"Indeed."

She waited for him to continue, and she was starting to feel as if she'd reached a natural point in the conversation that might allow her to find out exactly what Matthew Thorne expected.

"So I got your note," she said cautiously. "Obviously. And I called and arranged to come up here. I guess I'm really just wondering what made you invite me here tonight." Again she waited, trying to read some kind of answer in his expression. "It's not every night," she continued, "that some guy sees me alone at a bar and decides he wants to have me over for dinner. Most of them just have a hotel room upstairs somewhere, so that they can keep things anonymous."

"And how much do you make when you go with them?" he asked. "Humor me."

"It varies."

"What about the ones who want you to stay all night?"

She felt a shiver pass through her body.

"Everything's negotiable," she told him, figuring that she should continue to try to open the discussion up a little. "It depends on exactly what's expected. In my experience, everyone's got their own peccadilloes. I'm a very open-minded woman, and I just think it's best to be upfront about that sort of thing."

"I get the impression that you have a lot of

experience."

"I'm a fast learner," she replied, once again having to remember to breathe. "We're both adults. I'm sure we can come to some kind of agreement."

"As far as unusual situations go," he said softly, "I think this would be... unique."

"Again, I'm open to anything. More or less."

She waited, but she was starting to realize that Matthew required a little more prodding. That was fine, she'd met plenty of guys who lost a their courage when the moment arrived, and she was already trying to read the situation and figure out exactly how much control he wanted to cede. Finally, reaching down, she placed a hand on the side of his waist and offered a coy smile.

"Why don't you show me around the place?" she asked. "I'm sure a house like this must have a lot of empty rooms. A lot of empty bedrooms, in particular."

"We should eat first."

"Isn't dinner a couple of hours away?"

"And I've just poured the wine," he added.

"Okay," she said softly, keeping her hand on his waist, "I'm not going to hurry you, but I'll be ready when you are. All you have to do is let me know."

"I'll do that," he replied, as if he finally understood. "For now, how about I show you the downstairs areas while we finish this wine? The house is a real marvel and it's been so long since I've been able to give anyone a proper tour."

"That sounds like a great idea," she told him, pulling her hand away. "After all, you're in charge. We'll do whatever you want tonight."

CHAPTER TEN

"I BELIEVE THE HOUSE had been empty for a few years by the time I bought it," Matthew explained later, as he and Stella sat at either end of a long table in the dining room, with candles between them. "The previous owner was a shipping tycoon, something like that, who lost all his money on some racing team."

"So you just decided to move here to the South of France?" Stella asked.

"Well, my wife and I -"

Stopping himself suddenly, as if he'd said something that he'd intended to keep to himself, Matthew seemed momentarily frozen.

"Did you have to do a lot of work?" Stella continued, keen to avoid any further awkwardness. She figured that she didn't really need to delve into his private life, despite a sense of curiosity. "In terms of decoration, I mean."

"Some," he admitted cautiously. "The style isn't really my favorite, but any grand plans I might have had were rather stopped in their tracks when..."

Again, he seemed unable to finish the sentence.

"Things can get complicated," Stella suggested.

"How about you?" he asked. "What brought you to this part of the world?"

"I just fancied a change of scenery," she replied, bringing out the usual excuse that she always offered. "I suppose I'd just suffered through too many rainy English afternoons, and I decided I'd like to catch some sun."

"Dover can get pretty grim," he pointed out.

"Exactly," she said, although she was sure that she hadn't mentioned the fact that she'd lived for a while in Kent. She told herself that there was no harm if Matthew had carried out a little research. "I can't say I've ever really regretted that decision or -"

Before she could finish, she heard a bumping sound coming from somewhere upstairs. She looked up at the ceiling, and for a moment she felt certain that somebody must be in one of the other rooms. When she looked at Matthew, however, she saw a fearful expression in his eyes and she told herself that she probably shouldn't ask directly. At the same time, she needed to know whether or not they were truly alone.

"Don't," he said suddenly.

She looked back over at him.

"Don't worry, I mean," he continued. "There's no-one else here. Just you and me."

"I guess it's an old house, huh?" she replied, trying to make light of her concerns. "Lots of... old pipes?"

"Something like that."

"So do you work in some kind of... business?" she asked.

"I made my money in the markets," he explained, "but that was a long time ago. I was lucky with some investments, and I decided to get out and devote myself to humanitarian projects. I had this naive, idealistic belief that I could change the world for the better." He paused. "Unfortunately, as I'm sure you know all too well yourself, life has a habit of getting in the way and causing complications."

Not really knowing how to reply, Stella looked down at her plate. She'd never eaten scallops before, but she was finding them to be surprisingly tasty. At the same time, she was still having to remind herself to breathe all the time, and she couldn't help but worry that some interior mechanism had broken in her body. What if she had to remember to breathe for the rest of her life?

"My wife died less than a year after we arrived here," Matthew said, breaking the silence.

She looked at him again.

"We were so happy," he continued, "and she showed no signs of illness until... Well, until the moment she collapsed out there in the hallway, clutching her belly in agony. She was taken to the best doctors money can buy, I had her flown to Switzerland, but there was nothing they could do. The cancer had eaten its way through her body and gone completely undetected until right before the end. Sometimes I wonder whether she noticed that she was ill and kept it from me, but she swore she'd had no clue. Less than a week after she collapsed, she was dead."

"I'm so sorry," Stella replied. "What was her name?"

As soon as those words had left her lips, she regretted asking such an intrusive question.

"Martha," he said softly.

"That's really pretty."

"She had her whole life ahead of her," he said. "She was going to start a foundation dedicated to helping sick children in developing countries. She wanted to adopt, she was going to be the most wonderful mother and this house would have been filled with the sound of laughter and happiness, but..."

His voice trailed off for a moment.

"After she collapsed screaming," he added finally, "the place has never really been the same since."

"Have you considered moving?" Stella asked, feeling a little breathless now.

"I can't think of a single place I'd move *to*," he admitted. "I suppose I've somewhat stalled here at the mansion, and there's no motivation to leave. I just rattle around in the place, listening to the -"

He stopped abruptly, and Stella noticed that now he too was looking up toward the ceiling. She followed his gaze and saw another chandelier, but this time the house remained silent and there was no hint of another presence. It was at that moment, however, that Stella felt a creeping sense of fear starting to curl into her chest, and she realized that there might be another explanation for the sound she'd heard.

She'd always believed in ghosts, even if she'd never seen one. Now, as she watched the ceiling, she wondered whether something supernatural might be stalking the empty rooms of the large, mostly empty house.

"I shouldn't go on so much," Matthew said finally, as she looked back at him. "This is the last thing you want to hear over dinner, isn't it? Some rich asshole's sob story."

"No, it's fine," she told him. "People sometimes want to get things off their chests and..."

For a few seconds, she thought back to some of her previous clients, men who'd hired her by the hour but who'd simply wanted to talk about whatever was going on in their mundane lives. Most of them had told her stories that were pretty cliched, but she'd always managed to nod and express some kind of sympathy; this time, however, she was very much aware that the man sitting across from her was broken. Matthew Thorne had every opportunity that someone could want, yet he was frozen in time.

Suddenly a creaking sound rang out from the hallway, and Stella turned to look at the open door.

"Did you hear that?" Matthew asked.

She turned to him again.

"No," she stammered.

"Yes, you did," he replied. "I saw it in your eyes. Why would you deny something that's so obvious?"

"I don't know," she admitted, and she was feeling more and more uncomfortable as she forced herself to breathe in and out.

"Are you quite alright?" he asked.

"I'm just fine."

"You seem nervous. Out of breath."

"I said I'm fine," she said firmly, but his comments were only making her more aware of her struggle to breathe. "This food is really very nice. Did you make it yourself?" She flinched. "No, of course you didn't," she added, aware that she was rambling but unable to stop herself. "You already told me, you had a chef come in earlier and he left it out for you and..."

She finally managed to fall silent, and after a few seconds she swallowed hard.

"You heard the noise," Matthew said calmly. "I heard it too. I always hear. And the truth is, even after all this time, I don't quite know what to make of it."

"You don't?"

"When it's really bad," he continued, "that's when I go out to eat. Just for an hour or two. I don't usually like being around people, but there are times when I feel almost as if this place is suffocating me. Can you imagine what that's like?"

"No," she lied, shaking her head.

"I have a few glasses of wine in a restaurant," he added, "and by the time I come back here, I don't think I even notice the sounds anymore. That probably sounds rather pathetic, but it's the only thing I've ever really found that helps. Because otherwise, I stay up late, all alone in this house, and I start to wonder whether... just maybe... there might be a..."

Stella waited for him to finish that sentence.

"Money," he said suddenly.

"Money?"

"I should sort out the money side of things," he continued, suddenly getting to his feet as if he was in a panic. "That's how it's done, isn't it? We should keep this professional, rather than risk letting it slip into something murkier. I think it's important to define the edges of what we're doing here, so I'll go and fetch the money and then we can discuss business over the rest of dinner."

"Well, that's -"

"I insist," he added, hurrying out of the room as if he absolutely couldn't wait to leave. "Forgive me, I should have done this already. I almost forgot the correct order."

He muttered something else under his breath, but soon he was off in a distant part of the house, leaving Stella sitting all alone at the dining room table. She wasn't quite sure how to react to his sudden departure, but she quickly told herself that all guys were different and that Matthew had obviously been through a very difficult time. She hadn't quite pinned down a time frame, so she wasn't sure how long ago the man's wife had died, but evidently the pain was still very fresh. She figured she'd simply have to be sympathetic, and responsive to his needs, and avoid stepping on any toes.

Still having to think about each and every breath, she waited for Matthew Thorne to return.

CHAPTER ELEVEN

"HELLO?"

One hour later, stepping out from the dining room and looking across the large, ornate hallway, Stella listened out for any hint as to where Matthew might have gone. She'd waited and waited and waited, telling herself that he'd be back whenever he was ready, but now she was starting to worry that something might have happened to him. She listened for a few more seconds, and then she walked over to the middle of the hallway, hoping that the sound of her footsteps might be enough to draw him back.

Looking around, however, she began to wonder whether he'd left the house entirely.

"Hello?" she called out again. "Mr. Thorne? I'm sorry, I don't mean to bother you, it's just that I wanted to make sure that nothing's wrong and..."

She waited.

Silence.

Although she'd spent the previous hour continually telling herself that there was no need to worry, she couldn't help thinking that it was pretty strange – not to mention rude – for Matthew Thorne to simply abandon her. Then again, she was fairly sure that the guy had some serious issues, and she was starting to wonder whether she should just call it quits and find some way to get back to town. First, though, she wanted to try one final time to get through to her host and try to get the evening back on track. After all, she desperately needed the money.

Hearing a faint bump, she looked across the hallway and saw an open door, and after a few seconds she realized that there was a faint scuffing sound coming from one of the rooms.

"Hello?" she said cautiously as she made her way under the chandelier and over to the door. "Is -"

Stopping suddenly, she was surprised to see that Matthew Thorne was kneeling in front of a large, open safe. He seemed to be frozen in the process of taking out some money and – as she squinted to get a better look – Stella realized that she could see stack upon stack of cash on the safe's many shelves. She instantly tried to calculate just how much money was sitting there; even if the notes were the smallest in circulation, there had to be at least twenty or thirty thousand euros, possibly twice that, in which case there was more than enough to get her and Gary out of trouble forever. There was enough money to start a whole new life.

She could feel her heart pounding.

"I can't do this," Matthew whispered, clearly unaware that he was being overheard. He started to slowly rock back and forth. "Forgive me, but I'm just not strong enough."

Feeling as if she was intruding, Stella began to pull back, but at the last moment she realized that it might be useful to get a better idea of his state of mind.

"It's been so long," he continued, "and I thought I'd be ready, but how can *anyone* prepare for something like this? Every moment, every word, seems so raw and immediate. I can feel the awful end approaching and I know there's nothing I can do to stop it, so why do I keep hoping that I might come up with an idea? Why can't I just accept the inevitability of it all?"

Stella waited, but now the room fell silent, almost as if Matthew was listening to some quiet voice that only he could hear. Was it his wife? Was he having an imaginary conversation with the woman he loved? That thought broke Stella's heart, and she had to remind herself that the matter was really none of her business.

"I don't know if I'm ready," he added, "but I also don't think that I have a choice. This is how it's got to be, isn't it? There's not a man in history who could face up to this and not quake in his boots. How I wish that I'd never -"

He stopped, and after a moment he began to turn his head.

Keen to avoid being spotted, Stella immediately pulled back. She listened, but she heard nothing, certainly not the sound of footsteps approaching, so she turned and picked her way carefully across the hallway. She wasn't quite ready to write Matthew Thorne off as being completely insane, not yet, but she was becoming increasingly aware of his problems. In fact, she worried that any attempt to get him into bed might -

"Ms. Ward?"

Stopping in the doorway, Stella immediately realized that she'd been caught. She hesitated, trying to think of an excuse, and then she turned to see Matthew standing in the other doorway.

"Sorry," she said cautiously, unable to hide the fear in her voice, "I was just... looking for the bathroom."

"Forgive me," he replied, stepping forward, "I should have been a better host. There's a bathroom just to your left. Please, take as much time as you need."

"Thanks," she said, realizing that she was going to have to at least pretend to go into the room. She turned, but at that moment she saw a thick wad of cash in Matthew's left hand.

"This is for you," he explained, making his way toward her and holding the money out. "We didn't discuss a price, so I'm afraid I had to guess. If ten thousand for the night isn't enough, then just say and we can negotiate something more suitable."

"Ten... thousand?" she said, shocked to see so much money at once. "Euros?"

"I believe that's the prevailing currency," he replied, "although if you prefer to be paid in dollars or sterling, I can certainly do that. I hold multiple reserves."

"No, that's fine," she said, before she had a chance to stop herself. "It's absolutely great, I didn't mean to seem so flaky, it's just that I..."

"Really need that trip to the bathroom?" he suggested with a faint smile.

***

"You can do this," she whispered a few minutes later, leaning against the sink and staring at her reflection in the bathroom mirror. "Just don't think about the money. It's probably chickenfeed to a guy like him. He probably won't even notice he's spent it."

No matter how hard she tried to calm herself down, however, Stella felt a growing sense of panic in her chest. As she focused on breathing in and out, she was very much aware that her body desperately needed the oxygen, that even a couple of missed breaths would leave her feeling uncomfortable. The burden of having to take each breath – of having to *think* about each breath – was resting on her so heavily that she could barely think of anything else.

Finally, taking her phone from her purse, she switched it on with trembling hands and waited for the main screen to appear.

"You've done this sort of thing a million times before," she told herself, "and it's always gone fine. You have to get a grip."

She quickly saw that she had a number of missed calls from Gary, but she didn't have time to check her messages. Instead, she brought up his number and tapped to call, and then she waited for him to answer. All she wanted was to hear his voice telling her that there was no reason to panic, and that the ten thousand euros would go a long way toward dealing with all their problems.

"Pick up," she hissed, as the phone rang and rang. "Are you serious? You bugged me so much earlier, and *now* you decide to sulk?"

Either that, or he was blackout drunk again. For a moment she imagined him and his friends burning through more of their precious money at one of the many sleazy bars near the flat. She'd long since understood that she couldn't trust Gary with any level of responsibility, but she still felt as if her blood was starting to boil. He was the one who'd dragged them into such a difficult situation, and he was doing absolutely nothing to drag them back out.

She let the phone ring for a few more seconds, before cutting the line and slipping her phone away. She wasn't going to give Gary the satisfaction of leaving him loads of missed calls, and besides she worried that she'd already spent too long in the bathroom. She took a moment to check her makeup, and then she washed her hands. She knew deep down that she was delaying matters a little, but she also knew that there was no harm in keeping Matthew Thorne waiting for a few more minutes. After all, men tended to react passionately to a little frustration.

"Ten thousand euros," she told her reflection. "That's a hell of a payday, and who are you to argue if he thinks you're worth it? For that price, you just need to make sure that you show him a good time."

She took one last deep breath, just to make sure that her nerves were settled, and then she headed to the door.

CHAPTER TWELVE

"HEY," SHE SAID AS she reached the top of the stairs and saw Matthew standing with his back to her in the master bedroom, "I had a feeling this might be where I'd find you."

She waited for him to answer, and then – figuring that he was probably just a little shy and awkward – she made her way to the doorway. She knew she needed to appear sleek and attractive, and that the time had come to dispense with any caution and instead go straight to the heart of the matter. She had ten thousand euros in her purse, and she knew exactly what Matthew Thorne wanted in return, so she made her way up behind him and put her hands on the sides of his waist.

"That looks like a nice, big, comfortable bed," she whispered, watching the back of his head for any hint of a reaction. "Is that right? Is it the kind of bed someone could really get lost in?"

Again she waited, before stepping around and looking up into his eyes. He was staring at the bed, but she didn't let that fact deter her; instead, she reminded herself that he was paying her very handsomely to do a job, so she reached out and began to unbutton his shirt from the top.

"You're in charge, okay?" she told him. "There's nothing in this whole world you could say right now that would shock me. I have a *very* open imagination and your every wish is my command for this entire night. So how about I just get started, and then you let me know if you want something a little different?"

She opened another button, then another, revealing his bare chest.

"Does that sound like a good idea?" she asked, keeping her eyes fixed firmly on his face, waiting for him to look at her.

After a moment, she slipped a hand inside his shirt and touched his smooth, hot chest. Immediately, she realized she could feel his heart pounding against the undersides of her fingers. She was disappointed to find that he wasn't yet reacting to her attention in other ways, but she told herself that there was still plenty of time. As she leaned a little closer and moved in to kiss the side of her neck, she reminded herself that she was no psychologist; she was simply there to give him a good time for a few hours and hopefully put a smile on his face. Fixing him was somebody else's job.

Suddenly she spotted a woman standing out on the landing, staring straight at her with dark, ringed eyes.

"What the -"

Letting out a shocked gasp, Stella stepped back and bumped against the bed. She fell down, landing on the mattress, and then she leaned to the side and looked back over at the door. This time there was no sign of anyone on the landing, but the woman had been too clear, too distinct, to be a simple trick of the light.

"Are you okay?" Matthew asked.

"Who was that?" she stammered.

"What are you talking about?"

"Who *was* that?" she said again, before getting to her feet and hurrying to the door.

Even before she leaned out onto the landing, she knew that there'd be nobody there. Something about the woman's pale complexion and deathly glare had already convinced her that she'd looked into the face of a woman who was long dead.

"What did you see?" Matthew asked.

She turned to him, and in that moment she realized that she was trembling with fear.

"Tell me," he continued, and he didn't seem particularly shocked or surprised. Instead, he almost seemed resigned to what was happening. "Whatever it is, just tell me the truth."

"I saw..."

For a few seconds, she felt that she couldn't get the words out. How could she tell a man – especially a man like Matthew Thorne – that she thought she'd just seen the ghost of his dead wife?

"I don't know," she said finally, as her mind raced to come up with a convincing lie. "It was probably nothing. Just a shadow or..."

Her voice trailed off, and she could already tell that he was able to see right through her.

"I'm sorry," she continued, making her way back over to him, determined to pick up where she'd left off. "Please, I don't know what came over me but it won't happen again. I'm a professional."

"It's okay if you want to stop for a while," he told her. "If something scared you or -"

"No, I'm not scared," she said quickly, still feeling as if her heart was pounding. She looked past him and saw the empty landing, and she told herself that perhaps she *had* imagined the whole thing after all. "You know what it's like, right? The human mind can really play tricks on you."

She paused, and then she flinched a little as Matthew touched the side of her arm.

"Would you like another drink?" he asked.

"No," she replied, leaning closer, "I want to get started. I mean, I want to get to know you better."

She kissed him on the lips, forcing herself a little even as she felt that he was somewhat passive. When he still failed to respond after a few seconds, she put her hands on the side of his face and tried to make the kiss much more passionate; this time he joined in a little, although he still seemed somewhat reticent and she knew that she was going to have to find some way to shift him into a higher gear. As she pulled away, she told herself that she had to remember why she was there: she needed to give him what he wanted, and walk out the door with the ten thousand euros in her purse. And hadn't she always, deep down, felt that men were pretty easy to please?

"Here," she said, slipping her dress down a little further, "do you like that? Do you want me to take it off?"

"Do *you* want to take it off?" he asked.

"I want to do whatever you want me to do," she explained, trying to smile as she began to wonder whether he was really into her. "Your wish is my desire, and your desire is my wish, so all you have to do is..."

She slipped the dress down a little further, exposing more of her chest.

"You just have to tell me," she added softly, "and -"

"Wait!" he said suddenly, grabbing her

hand. "I need to... freshen up. I'm sorry, do you mind? I'll only be a couple of minutes."

"Sure," she lied, trying to not let on that she was disappointed. "Whatever you want."

"I'll be back soon," he added, taking a step away and then heading toward the door. He seemed a little distracted and, as he made his way out of the room, he reached out and brushed a hand against the door's side, almost as if he was feeling a little weak. He murmured something under his breath, something Stella wasn't quite able to make out, and then he was gone.

"Okay," she said, a little unsure of herself as she looked at the mirror on the far wall and saw her reflection with her dress partly pulled down.

Figuring that she needed to reset, she wandered over to the mirror and took a moment to put her dress straight. She was starting to worry that Matthew Thorne wouldn't be able to go through with the night's activities; she felt bad for him, but she told herself that he seemed like a decent guy and that he'd almost certainly let her keep the money regardless. After all, he was still using her time, even if they weren't doing quite what she'd expected.

Still looking into the mirror, she watched the space over her shoulder. She could see the reflection of the bed, but she wasn't quite able to shake the feeling that she was being watched. She turned and looked, worried that the ghostly woman might make a reappearance, and then she told herself that she needed to calm down. With each passing second, she found it a little easier to convince herself that she'd imagined the whole thing, and she figured that the strange atmosphere of the house was simply getting to her.

Realizing that Matthew seemed to be really taking his time, she walked back over to the end of the bed and sat down. She wasn't quite sure how to deal with such a tricky customer, but she wasn't the kind of person who let herself get defeated so easily; she was already trying to think up a few new ideas that might stir key parts of his anatomy. One possibility was to simply strip off and make sure that when Matthew returned, there could be no more delays or ambiguities.

And then, slowly, she began to realize that she could hear a faint sound nearby. Somebody was behind her, breathing heavily. She began to turn, only to stop herself at the last second as she began to worry that she was giving in to her fears. The breathing sound continued, inching closer, and a moment later she felt the bed shift slightly as if some other weight had begun to press down at the top.

Taking a big, deep breath, Stella told herself that the sound would stop if she could just think about something else.

Suddenly a hand touched her shoulder. Unable to stop herself, she turned and saw to her horror that the woman – deathly thin and pale now – was leaning toward her and letting out a long, guttural gasp.

CHAPTER THIRTEEN

"STELLA?" MATTHEW CALLED AFTER her. "Stella, what's wrong?"

"I have to go!" she blurted out, racing down the stairs so fast that she almost tripped with each step.

Too scared to look back, convinced that she'd see the awful woman again, she hurried to the front door before stopping as she realized that she'd forgotten her purse. She looked around, frantically trying to remember where she'd set it down earlier, and then she remembered that she'd placed it on the dining table after putting the cash away.

"Stella," Matthew continued as she rushed to the dining room, "can you please tell me what's going on?"

Her hands were trembling as she grabbed

the purse. It immediately fell open and all the contents threatened to spill out; somehow she managed to clip it shut again and run back out to the hallway, but her sense of panic was escalating rapidly. This time she glanced up the stairs and saw Matthew standing at the top, staring down at her with a bemused expression. There was no sign of the woman, not this time, but she wasn't going to take any chances.

"I have to get out of here," she stammered, rushing to the door and pulling it open. "I'm sorry, I can't -"

Before she could finish, the purse fell from her hand and hit the floor. Turning, she saw that the clasp had failed again, and she watched in horror as her make-up and phone and the wad of cash spilled out; the cash, in particular, separated and fanned out across the marble until some of the notes hit the bottom of the staircase.

"Damn it!" she muttered under her breath, dropping to her knees and grabbing her phone and lipstick, then reaching for some of the money. "I'm sorry," she added, looking up at Matthew again, "I just -"

She froze as soon as she saw the dead woman standing at the top of the stairs, just behind Matthew. For a moment, Stella could only stare at the woman as she felt a chill starting to spread throughout her body. She knew she was looking at something unnatural, something that went against everything she thought she understood about the world, something that seemed somehow to be radiating death throughout the house with such force that – finally – she began to fear that she was at risk of catching something from the air.

"I..."

She tried to speak, but now she knew she had only one option.

Grabbing her phone and empty purse, and leaving the money behind, she scrambled to her feet and raced out through the open front door.

***

She ran and ran, until finally she reached the large iron gate and tried to pull it open, only to find that it was firmly locked. She pulled a couple more times, hoping to somehow force the mechanism, and then she looked at the wall. She could see a row of spikes on the top, but she told herself that she'd just have to be careful as she began to climb to freedom.

Reaching the top, she maneuvered over the spikes, which turned out to not be as sharp as she'd feared. She caught herself a couple of times, but not hard enough to draw blood, and then she threw herself over the other side and dropped down onto the grass, landing hard and immediately toppling over. Letting out a pained gasp as she slammed down, she immediately began to get up, at which point she allowed herself to look back at the house.

She could see a figure standing at the top of the steps, watching her escape. For a moment she wanted to call out to Matthew and tell him what she'd seen, but instead she turned and began to hurry away along the road that led back toward Nice.

The lights of the city glittered in the distance.

With each step, Stella felt herself once again having to remember to breathe. She was struggling a little, perhaps because she was walking so quickly but perhaps also because she was in the throes of panic. Each breath seemed harder than the last, as if she was really having to work her lungs, and she couldn't help but worry that soon she'd find the effort far too difficult. Each breath seemed to come at a great cost.

Reaching into her purse, she pulled out her phone and struggled with shaking hands to switch it back on and bring up Gary's number. She glanced over her shoulders a couple of times, to make sure that there was no sign of anyone following her, and then she tapped to call.

"Please pick up," she whimpered, as tears began to run down her cheeks. "Please..."

As she waited, she looked at the lights of Nice in the distance, down by the sea. She knew that making the journey on foot would take at least three hours, maybe longer, so she quickly stopped and removed her heels before setting off again. She could feel sheer terror rumbling in the pit of her stomach, but she tried to reassure herself that if there *was* a ghost at Matthew Thorne's house, it couldn't reach her now.

She still glanced over her shoulder a couple more times, just to be sure that she was alone, before hurrying around a bend in the road.

"What the hell is wrong with you?" she muttered as the call was diverted to Gary's voicemail.

She tapped to cut the call, and then she tried him again.

"I'm not going to stop," she said out loud, trying to find some strength from somewhere. She could hear the breathlessness in her own voice. "I'm going to keep calling you until you pick up, you bastard!"

Once again, however, she was put through to his voicemail. She cut the call and prepared to try for a third time, only for the phone to suddenly start ringing. She didn't recognize the number, so she hesitated before tapping to accept the call.

She listened, and for a moment she heard nothing.

"Stella?" Matthew Thorne said finally, his voice filled with concern. "Can we talk? You ran out of here so fast and I'm worried about you. And you left the money behind. Please, at least let me pay you."

She wanted to ask him what was happening in his house, but already she was starting to notice another sound on the line. She could hear Matthew breathing, but she could also hear a faint, low gasp that immediately reminded her of the woman she'd seen in the bedroom. Either Matthew Thorne didn't mind the fact that a ghost was with him, or he hadn't noticed the strange sound.

"Stella," he continued, "say something. At least tell me that you're okay. I can send a car, someone will drive you home. I can't possibly let you walk the whole way. For one thing, it's not safe, and for another it's going to take you hours. Please, at least accept this small offer of help from me."

Instead of replying, Stella simply listened as the breathing sound continued. Whoever or whatever was with Matthew on the other end of the line, it seemed to be slowly getting closer to the phone, and she couldn't help but imagine the dead woman standing right next to him in the house's grand hallway. She wanted to ask him if he really couldn't hear what was happening, but she wasn't sure how to get the words out without sounding like a complete fool.

Suddenly the gasping sound stopped, and Stella swallowed hard.

"When you get to the junction," Matthew said, "wait and a car will arrive. It might be half an hour or so, but it'll be there as soon as possible, and I want you to at least let me send you back to wherever you live. That's the least I can do."

Although she briefly considered taking him up on his offer, deep down Stella felt that she couldn't possibly accept any of his help. The last thing she wanted was to risk any further connection to Matthew Thorne, so after a few more seconds she cut the call and slipped her phone away. Then, looking over her shoulder toward the distant gate, she realized she could see a figure standing in the darkness by the side of the road.

She watched the figure, trying to make out any of its details, but a moment later the cloud cover lifted slightly; a little moonlight illuminated the scene, and in an instant the figure was gone.

"Keep away from me," Stella called out, unable to stop herself. "I don't want anything to do with you!"

She looked around, just in case there was any chance that it might return, and then she hurried away along the road. When she reached the junction she immediately set off down the hill, while trying to figure out a less obvious route that would help her avoid Matthew Thorne's driver.

All she wanted to do was get home and forget that she'd ever set foot in that house at all.

AMY CROSS

CHAPTER FOURTEEN

BY THE TIME SHE reached the alley and saw the door to the flat, morning sunlight was starting to spread through the city's streets. Stopping for a moment, feeling the soreness of her bare feet, Stella suddenly noticed that her breathing had returned to normal; she'd been breathing without thinking since some point on the walk home.

For the first time, she felt as if she'd finally left Matthew Thorne's creepy house far behind.

Sighing, she picked her way carefully along the alley. The tarmac wasn't particularly comfortable against the soles of her bare feet, but she knew her heels would be worse. As she reached the flat's front door, however, she saw that it had been left partly open, and that the area around the lock appeared to have been smashed. Her first thought was that the place must have been burgled while she was away, but – as she stopped in the doorway and looked through to the interior – she began to realize that there might be another explanation.

Cole and his gang.

"Gary?" she called out cautiously, hoping against hope that he hadn't been home while anything bad was happening. "Gary, are you here?"

She made her way through to the front room, but all she saw was more damage. The flat had been trashed and she was starting to feel increasingly sure that something very bad had happened while she'd been away.

"Where are you?" she muttered, grabbing her phone again, filled with concern for Gary's safety. "I swear, if you've got yourself into even more trouble..."

***

"I haven't seen Gary for weeks," Jordan explained as he set some more empty glasses on a shelf behind the bar. "Why, what's he managed to get himself involved with this time?"

"He's probably just sleeping a big night off on someone's sofa," Stella replied, trying to not sound too concerned. "You know what he's like when he really goes off on one."

Jordan glanced at her, and she immediately knew that he wasn't buying a word of her attempt to bluff.

"You could always go to the police," he suggested with a grin. "If you're worried, I mean."

"You know I can't do that."

"They're still after him, are they?"

"It's complicated, but he's trying to get clean."

"What if he's using again?"

"He wouldn't do that."

"Once a junkie, always a -"

"He wouldn't do it!" she snapped, unable to contain a burst of anger. "I told you, he's clean now."

She hated the fact that her voice was filled with desperation.

"You said he's trying to *get* clean," he pointed out. "That's a different thing. You've got no idea how many people I've met in this business who say they're going to sort themselves out, only for them to end up back in the gutter. Or worse."

"I have to go," she replied, turning to leave before stopping for a moment. "Do you know anything about this Cole guy that Gary got himself involved with?"

"I stay away from that sort of thing," Jordan told her. "There are certain things that go on around this place that I don't want anything to do with. I run a decent bar here and I'm not going to change that by letting a bunch of smackheads start using it. That's why I barred Gary and his mates a long time ago."

"You barred them?"

"He didn't tell you? Now there's a shocker."

"I really have to go," she said, and this time she hurried away across the empty bar, quickly emerging onto the bright morning street.

Stopping, she used a hand to shield her eyes as she looked both ways. She was hoping for a miracle, for Gary to suddenly slink into view nursing a massive hangover. He'd disappeared before, sometimes for days at a time, and she usually just rolled her eyes and waited for him to show up. This time felt different, however, and she couldn't help but worry that Cole's thugs might have decided to make a move early.

Setting off along one of the streets, she tried to stay calm, although a couple of people cast concerned glances in her direction and she was starting to wonder whether she looked upset. She managed to smile back at most of the people, but she quickly made her way down a side street in an attempt to get away from the crowds of tourists. Spotting a jewelry store ahead, she told herself that she simply needed to go home and wait for Gary to show up. As she reached the corner and turned, however, she glanced at the store's window and froze as soon as she saw her reflection.

The dead woman was standing right behind her.

Startled, she spun around and slammed back against the wall. There was no sign of the woman now, but Stella's heart was pounding as she looked both ways along the street. Once she was sure that there really was no-one nearby, she took a step forward, and then she forced herself to look at her reflection again.

This time, she saw only her own terrified face staring back.

"Are you okay?"

Shocked again, she turned to see that a man was watching her from a nearby doorway. Old and wearing a shirt that was almost completely open at the front, the man took a drag from his cigarette while eyeing her up and down.

"English, yes?" he continued with a faint smile. "I can always tell. You English look out of place wherever you go."

"Did you see someone just now?" she asked.

The man tilted his head.

"Did you see someone with me?" she continued, unable to hide the fear in her voice. "When I walked down this street, was I alone or..."

Her voice trailed off as she began to realize that she sounded insane.

"It's the heat," she added, wiping sweat from

her brow as she once again looked round to make sure that the woman was gone. "It's getting to me."

"I didn't see anyone," the man told her. "All I saw was you, and it looked like you got a hell of a fright. You're right about the heat, it'll get you in ways you never expect. If you want my advice, you'll sit down somewhere in the shade and get some water down you. Nothing good ever came of rushing about in the daytime."

"I know," she murmured, before turning and hurrying away. "I'm sorry."

Reaching the next street, which was even narrower and tighter than the last, she began to make her way past various apartment buildings. She told herself over and over that there was no need to panic, that she was letting her imagination run wild, but she could feel her heart thudding harder and harder in her chest, and she was starting to worry that she was no longer in control of her own body. It was as if her meat and bones were forcing her to run, even as her mind tried to stay calm.

Suddenly she stopped as she heard a snarling sound. For a moment, too dazed to understand what was happening, she looked around, but finally she spotted a dog sitting nearby on a pile of garbage. The dog appeared to have been sleeping, but now it was baring its teeth as it slowly stood and stepped closer. Although she couldn't quite tell the dog's breed, Stella pulled back against the wall as the large animal padded toward her, until at the last moment she realized that it wasn't snarling at *her* at all.

Instead, the dog seemed angered by something that was next to her, although when she looked to her left she saw nothing nearby.

She flinched as the dog started barking.

"It's okay," she stammered, turning and holding her hands up. "I'm not going to hurt you. See? I'm a friend, I'm just passing by."

With saliva dripping from its gums, the dog bared its fangs and barked again.

"I'm sorry," Stella said, hurrying past and almost tripping over her own feet as she made her way along the street. "Please, just leave me alone..."

Reaching the next corner, she looked back and saw that the dog was following, but that it still seemed to be angry at some invisible foe. The hair on the dog's back was standing up, and Stella felt for a moment as if she could see real madness in the animal's eyes. As she tried to stay calm, she began to worry that the creature might be rabid.

"I'm sorry," she said again, before turning to run, "I really didn't mean to disturb you."

As soon as she got to the end of the next street, she looked back and saw to her relief that the dog had turned away. She watched as it returned to its position outside one of the buildings, and then she leaned back for a moment against the wall. She could feel the sun beating relentlessly against her forehead, and sweat was running down her face, but a few seconds later the air was pierced by a horrific, high-pitched scream that rang out from a nearby street.

CHAPTER FIFTEEN

AS SIRENS BLARED, STELLA stepped around another corner and saw that several police cars had stopped at a nearby junction. A small crowd had begun to gather, and two ambulances were pulling up just a few meters away.

"What happened?" she asked, craning her neck to try to see through the crowd. "Is someone hurt?"

"Some drug addict," a woman muttered nearby, with obvious disgust in her voice. "Another useless young man. I don't know what they think they're doing, but someone should run them out of town. We don't want vermin here."

"Is he hurt?"

"There was some shouting and a chase," the woman explained. "I think one of them ran out into traffic and tripped." She turned to Stella. "I heard the crunch. I think he went straight under the wheels of a bus." She sighed heavily. "I know he was some mother's son, but still, it's no great loss, is it? I wish all those drug addicts and dealers would get out of here. They're just a drain on everyone else."

"Excuse me," Stella said, trying to slip past people who'd gathered to watch the scene. "I'm sorry, I really need to get through."

No matter how hard she tried to tell herself that Gary would be fine, that there was no way he'd be caught up in some kind of argument in the middle of the day, she was once again feeling an overwhelming sense of panic as she forced herself to the front of the crowd. She could hear the chatter of police radios, and a voice was shouting for everyone to stay back, but a moment later Stella saw a bus over on the far side of the street with several officers gathered around the front. In that instant, she felt a crushing sense of panic in the center of her chest, pushing so hard that she was struggling to breathe.

Suddenly another officer stepped in front of her and held his hands up, saying something in French about her having to stand back.

"I need to see if it's him," she said, peering first one way and then the other around the officer as he tried to push her back into the crowd. "You don't understand, I need to be sure."

The officer continued to talk to her in French, saying things she didn't quite understand, and a moment later she realized she could just about make out a figure trapped under the bus. She couldn't see much detail, but the figure was wearing dark clothes, which was how Gary had been dressed when she'd last seen him more than twelve hours earlier.

"I need to look!" she hissed, as more police cars stopped nearby. "Why won't you let me look? I have to make sure it's not him!"

The officer tried again to shove her back. This time, Stella ducked down and rushed past him. Ignoring several raised voices that were yelling at her in French, she ran across the street and slipped between two other officers, and then she stopped as she spotted the body on the ground. For a moment, all she saw was a mess of blood and flesh and hair, wrapped in torn fabric, and she struggled to tell exactly which part was which until – finally – she was able to make out an arm and a chest.

A police officer tried to pull her back, but she refused to go. She could hear voices shouting at her, but they were somehow fading into the background as she heard the sound of her own labored breaths.

The dead man's head had been crushed, with part of his skull trapped beneath a wheel. The wheel itself was caked in blood and bone, and had left a trail of smeared flesh across the road. Fresh blood glistened in the sunlight, and pieces of broken bone were poking out through the side of the head like a dislodged crown. The man's face was impossible to make out, but his right hand bore several old tattoos, and Bella let out a sigh of relief as she realized that it wasn't Gary.

"It's not him," she whispered, with tears of joy in her eyes. "It's really not him..."

For one brief moment, everything seemed right with the world.

Grabbing her arm, a police officer suddenly pulled her away while saying something in French, but Stella could only let out a cry of relief, and then she started laughing as she looked around to see whether Gary was nearby.

"I have to go," she said finally, horrified by her own reaction, and she quickly pulled away from the police officer and hurried into the crowd. "I'm sorry, I didn't mean to laugh, I was just so relieved."

She could feel her face burning now as the sun seemed to become so much more intense. She looked around, wondering why everyone else seemed to be fine, and then she spilled out at the back of the crowd and stopped to steady herself outside a money-changing kiosk. Struggling to get her breath back, she heard more sirens, and then she turned to see a man sitting nearby on the floor, leaning against the wall. She wasn't sure why, but something about the man immediately caught her attention, and she couldn't help but notice that he was watching the crowd with a curiously blank expression.

And then he turned and looked up at her.

"Who are you?" he asked.

"I'm sorry?" she replied.

"Who are you?" he asked again. "Why did you have to look?"

"I don't know what you -"

"Why did you have to look at me?" he continued, as a hint of anger began to creep into his tone. "No-one should have to be seen when they're in a state like that. Why did you have to come and stare at me? You're just like all the rest. Don't you have any sense of decency?"

"I really don't know what you're talking about," she replied, even as she felt a cold shiver run through her bones. "I don't even know who you are."

"I'm pretty sure you do," he told her, as a bead of blood began to run down from his hairline, trickling across his cheek. "I can see you. I know your eyes are open now."

"I don't -"

"You got a good look at me, huh?" he continued. "Yeah, I saw you, you got a good look at me inside and out. Did that push your buttons? Did you get a little buzz out of it?"

She shook her head.

"You seemed pretty happy," he added. "I could see it in your eyes. You didn't care about what had happened to me. All you cared about was that I wasn't someone else. Don't pretend that you give a damn, because I know you don't! No-one does!"

"I'm only -"

Before she could finish, Stella realized that the man's head was starting to collapse on one side. She heard a crunching sound, and to her horror she saw that part of his forehead was crushing inward, allowing sharp pieces of bone to rip through the skin as his eye socket ruptured and his left eyeball split down the middle. The man's body was breaking down right in front of her, and all she could do was stare in horror.

"I think you know exactly who I am," the man said, slowly getting to his feet as his jaw began to crack open. He managed a couple more words, but blood was already gushing from his lips and after a moment he lurched forward and tried to grab Stella's arm.

"No!" she shouted, pulling away and bumping against the glass front of the kiosk. She knew that people were staring at her now, but she didn't understand why they too weren't horrified by the sight of the man.

He tried again to speak, but now his head was almost completely crushed, just as it had appeared when his body had been trapped beneath the bus.

"Leave me alone!" Stella screamed, turning to run but immediately bumping against another woman.

"Are you okay?" the woman asked.

"He's alive!" she stammered. "I don't know how, but somehow he got out from under the bus!"

"What are you talking about?"

Stella opened her mouth to reply, but at that moment she looked over her shoulder and saw that the man was gone. She turned the other way, convinced that he had to be close, and then she looked over toward the bus just in time to see some paramedics placing a sheet over the corpse. She felt a rush of relief that at least she knew the body hadn't belonged to Gary, but at the same time she was trying to work out whether she'd actually been speaking to a dead man.

"Do you want me to call someone for you?" the woman said, clearly concerned. "Are you on holiday?"

"I'm fine," Stella murmured, pushing her hand away before turning and hurrying past the crowd as more and more sirens filled the air. "I'm going to be okay. I just need to find Gary."

CHAPTER SIXTEEN

BY THE TIME NIGHT began to fall again, Stella still hadn't gone back to the flat. She'd spent the entire day on her feet, walking the streets of the city, desperately searching for Gary. She'd tried to call him, she'd tried all his old haunts, and now she was resorting to desperate measures.

Her soles were worn and bloodied, and caked in grime.

"Have you seen Gary?" she asked for the thousandth time, barely able to get the words out as she walked along the street. She wasn't even asking anyone in particular; she was simply putting the call out into the world, hoping that someone would answer. "He's my boyfriend. Has anyone seen him?"

Her legs were so tired, they could barely

carry her. Still, she walked over to some tables outside a restaurant, hoping against hope that somebody there might actually know Gary and might have seen him during the day. She'd reached the point of begging for miracles.

"Have any of you seen Gary?" she stammered, even as the restaurant's customers stared back at her with bemused expressions. "Do you know if he's okay?"

Realizing that they didn't know what she was talking about, she turned to cross the road. At that moment, looking up, she saw lights in the distance and she realized that Matthew Thorne's house was still out there somewhere in the darkness beyond the edge of town. She thought of Matthew rattling around in all those empty rooms, and a shiver passed through her body as she remembered the sight of the dead woman. She'd been in a real haunted house, she'd met a real ghost and a real haunted man. She'd been on the verge of entering a ghost story.

After a moment, however, she reminded herself that she had to stay focused on Gary, so she wandered to the restaurant, only for a waiter to step in front of her and tell her to leave.

"I just need to ask them about Gary," she explained, but she could already tell that she wasn't welcome.

Walking past the restaurant, she emerged in

a small square and saw one of the bars that she and Gary had sometimes visited when they'd first arrived in Nice. She couldn't remember whether she'd been there recently, so she made her way over, convinced that someone somewhere in the city had to know something about Gary's whereabouts.

The bar was fairly busy already, but she made her way past the smattering of customers and approached the bar, where Jordan had just finished serving a couple of women.

"Back again, huh?" he muttered, glancing at her with a hint of caution in his eyes. "Twice in one day. That makes me a lucky man, I suppose."

"I haven't been here since..."

Her voice trailed off as she began to realize that perhaps she *had* been to Jordan's bar earlier in the day. Everything seemed vague and unfocused, and the entire room was swimming all around her as if it existed in a slightly different world.

"Have you seen Gary?" she murmured.

"Not since the last time you asked."

"When was the last time I asked?"

"About two seconds ago," he replied. "You've asked me that half a dozen times since you walked through the door."

"No, I haven't," she said, shaking her head, convinced that he had to be wrong.

"Are you on something, Stella?" he continued. "You know my policy on stuff like that,

I'm going to have to ask you to leave if you're on drugs."

"I'm not on drugs," she told him, as she reached out to steady herself against the bar. The pounding music seemed to be reaching inside her head. "I've never done drugs, you know that."

"If -"

"My dad died of a heart attack years ago," she added, slurring her words a little. "There's a heart condition in my family. I always swore I'd never abuse my body like that."

"Then you should go home," he told her. "You don't look too hot. You should go home and get some rest, and look after yourself a little bit."

"Not until I've found Gary."

"Well, he's not here," he pointed out. "I don't know what rock he's crawled under, but he'll crawl out again soon enough. People like that always do."

"I have to find him," she said, turning to walk away.

"Your friend earlier looked like a druggie," he added. "She had that kind of lost expression I've seen so many times before."

"What friend?" she asked cautiously, turning back to him. "I wasn't with anyone when I came earlier."

"Uh, yeah, you were," he said, rolling his eyes. "Freaky looking girl. Well, I say *girl*, she looked a bit older than you and she was... I don't know how to describe it, but she didn't look right. She gave me the creeps, the way she was just standing a little way behind you and staring at you."

"I was alone," she told him, struggling to hide her sense of panic. "I remember now, I know I was here, but I was by myself."

"No, there was a woman with you," he said matter-of-factly. "She had really dark eyes, I think she was wearing some kind of make-up to make herself look crazy. She followed you in, she stood around while you talked to me, and then she followed you out. I almost wondered if she was some weirdo who was just stalking you, but then she talked to you as you left, and you didn't really seem to react."

"What..."

Stella thought back to her earlier visit. She was remembering more and more details now, but she still felt certain that she'd been alone.

"What was she saying to me?"

"Something about Gary, I think," he told her, as some more girls approached the bar. "Or some guy, anyway. She was telling you to keep away from him. She didn't seem angry, though. It was more like she was slightly stoned."

"There was no woman with me!" Stella snapped, trying not to panic. "Why are you lying?"

Ignoring her, Jordan began to serve the other

two women.

Stella hesitated for a moment, before slipping her phone out and seeing that she had a small amount of battery left. With trembling fingers, she realized that there was one thing she could do, one thing she'd been too scared to try earlier. She brought up a search page, and then she entered Matthew Thorne's name. She couldn't remember the name of his wife, but she began to try to find some record. Sure enough, she quickly discovered plenty of news stories about Matthew and his philanthropic efforts, and many of the articles mentioned his wife as well.

"Martha," Stella whispered as she scrolled down the page, desperately searching for a photo. "Martha Thorne."

Suddenly she saw a photo showing Matthew and his wife at some fancy gala, and she immediately froze as she realized that she recognized the woman. Sure, the Martha Thorne in the picture looked happy and healthy, glowing even, as she posed for photographs, while the woman at the house had been painfully thin and sickly, but there was no doubting the fact that they were one and the same person. The more she stared at the image, the more Stella tried to convince herself that there was some kind of mistake, yet she could feel a growing sense of acceptance creeping into her heart. A moment later she spotted a link to another news story, and this one mentioned Martha Thorne's sudden death a few years earlier.

"This is impossible," she said, before hurrying back over to Jordan and holding the phone up for him to see. "Is this her?"

"Hang on," he replied, still dealing with the other customers.

"Is this her?" Stella snapped, pushing the women aside.

"Watch it!" one of the women snarled, pushing her back. "Wait your turn, you stupid bitch!"

"Is this the woman you saw with me?" Stella asked, even though she was absolutely terrified of the answer.

Jordan reached out to push the phone away, but then he hesitated for a moment as he peered at the screen.

"Yeah, that's her," he admitted finally. "She looked a hell of a lot worse this morning, but it's definitely her. Listen, Stella, I can't have you making a scene in here. If you're not going to have a drink, and I strongly suggest that you shouldn't, then I really think it's time for you to head home. Wait for Gary there. He'll wash up eventually."

Feeling a little short of breath now, Stella took a couple of steps back before bumping against a table. Startled, she spun around, looking for any sign of Martha Thorne's dead face, and then she turned to Jordan again.

"Do you see her?" she shouted.

"Stella -"

"Do you see her now?" she screamed. "Just tell me! Do you see her here with me right now?"

"No," Jordan replied, as the other customers stared at her as if she'd completely lost her mind. "Stella, seriously, you're making a right tit of yourself. Go home and sleep off... whatever the hell this is."

Looking around yet again, Stella saw lots of face staring at her, but there was no sign of Martha Thorne. She wanted to explain what was happening, to tell them all that she wasn't crazy, even though she could think of no way to put her experience into words. Finally, worried that she might be about to faint, she turned and ran out of the loud club and off into the dark, busy Nice night.

CHAPTER SEVENTEEN

SOMEHOW, AFTER WALKING FOR many more hours, Stella found herself back outside the flat. She wasn't sure whether she'd subconsciously headed in that direction, or whether her route had been genuinely random, but – as she looked along the alley and saw the flat's broken front door – she realized that she couldn't simply start wandering again. The sun was rising yet again, even though she wasn't sure quite where all the hours had gone. Exhausted and on the verge of collapse, she stumbled toward the flat and pushed the door open.

As soon as she stepped into the hallway, she heard a faint bumping sound coming from one of the other rooms.

"Hello?" she called out.

She waited, and the sound continued.

"If someone's there, you'd better show yourself," she continued, before grabbing one of Gary's old golf clubs from behind the door and holding it up as a weapon. "I want to know where Gary is! Do you understand? I want..."

Her voice trailed off as she began to realize that another presence might be waiting for her.

"I just want to be left alone," she added, imagining Martha Thorne's ghostly figure in the front room. "I just -"

Before she could finish, she heard a faint groan coming from one of the rooms. Still holding the golf club, she hurried through, and to her horror she saw Gary slumped bloodied and battered in one of the armchairs.

"What happened?" she gasped, racing over and dropping to her knees, and immediately seeing that he had not only a broken nose but also two black eyes. "Gary, did Cole's men do this to you?"

He tried to push her away, but she took hold of his head and forced him to look at her.

"You need to see a doctor," she told him. "Now."

"It's okay," he said, slurring his speech a little. "They just wanted to convey a message, that's all. Which they did, quite effectively. They're -"

He winced as he tried to sit up. After pausing for a moment, he tried again, and this time he just about managed.

"They're running out of patience," he continued, as he rubbed the side of his face. "The problem with men like Cole is that they like getting their money back, but they also like making examples of people every now and then. If I don't have the full fifty grand for him by midnight tonight, he'll..."

His voice trailed off, and then he managed a faint, pained smile as he looked at her.

"Hey, you're so beautiful," he said, allowing himself a brief chuckle. "Tell me about your night. You were gone a long time. Wait, was that last night or the night before? My head's a little woozy. How much did you make?"

"Gary -"

"I hope it was a lot," he added, "because we really need that money, Stella. I mean, we *really* need it. It's life or death. For me, at least. I've managed to keep you out of it."

"We have to go to the police."

"Don't talk stupid."

"They'll do something!" she insisted. "Enough's enough, we can't let a gang of criminals keep threatening us!" She waited for him to agree. "I know we'll get into trouble, I accept that, but it's a price worth paying if it means we can start fresh in a year or two. I can handle prison, Gary, but I can't handle losing you!"

"It's too late," he said, shaking his head.

"How much did you make at that rich dude's house?"

"I..."

She paused for a moment, thinking back to the sight of the money she'd dropped.

"I had some cash," she admitted, "but... I can't really explain, it's a long story. Everything turned kind of crazy and I had to run, so I lost all the money. There was ten grand, but it's gone."

"Ten grand?" He smiled, and this time he seemed genuine, although after a moment tears reached his eyes. "That's enough for you to get out of town, Stella," he continued. "It's me these guys are after, not you. Not really. I'm going to tell them that you had nothing to do with it all, and I'll make sure that I'm the one who pays. You just get that ten grand and head off into the distance and don't look back."

"I'm not leaving you!" she said firmly, and now she too was on the verge of breaking down. "I love you!"

"It's the end of the road, Stella," he replied, his voice drained off all emotion. "The clock's ticking. If there's only one thing left for me to do before they get me, then I'm going to make sure that you're alright. You're the only thing that matters to me now in the whole world."

***

Several hours later, sitting on some rocks near the edge of the beach, Stella watched as happy families played in the sand and the water. She envied them, but she also hated them, and she was trying to work out how – at only twenty-four years of age – her life was already so completely ruined.

Mid-morning sunlight glittered on the sea.

Hearing footsteps, she turned just in time to see that Gary was on his way back from seeing his 'friend'. His face was patched up to some degree, although he still looked rough, and Stella's heart broke as she saw the pained expression on his features.

"Okay, I looked into a few things," he said, clutching a handful of papers. "Because of Brexit and a load of other stuff, you're better off staying in France. Don't try Italy or anywhere like that, because you won't have the right to stay permanently." He held the papers out to her. "You need to go north and head to somewhere on the west coast."

"I'm not leaving you," she said, ignoring the papers in his hand. "How many times do I have to tell you that?"

"I can deal with everything that's coming to me," he replied, "but only if I truly know that you're going to be fine. If I know that you're on a bus or a train to somewhere like La Rochelle."

He reached out and moved some hair from across her face.

"You can have a good life there," he continued, offering a pained smile. "Just forget about me. Forget about all of this. The only thing that matters is you."

"If we can find the money -"

"We can't find fifty grand in twelve hours," he told her. "Even *I'm* not that optimistic. And Cole won't accept anything less than the full amount."

She opened her mouth to argue with him, and then she hesitated for a few seconds. She hadn't had time to go into detail with him about everything that had happened at Matthew Thorne's house, but now she was thinking back to the sight of all the cash in his safe. Every time she tried to figure out how much money had been sitting on those shelves, she came to the same conclusion, which was that there had to be more than enough to cover Gary's debts and get them both out of trouble. She knew that Matthew Thorne was a complex individual, but she felt certain that there had to be some way to make him cut a deal.

"I've got an idea," she said finally.

"The only idea you should be having right now is to get to the train station and -"

"I know where to find fifty thousand euros in cash," she continued, interrupting him as she watched some children playing in the sea. "It's just sitting there in Matthew Thorne's safe, and I think he might give it to me if I find the right way to ask."

He turned to her.

"I'm serious," she added. "He was ready to give me ten grand just for an overnighter."

"Yeah, but you said he flaked out."

"It's a bit more complicated than that," she explained, "but the point is, I think he's a decent guy. And I think there might be some way to get through to him, to make him understand that we really need his help."

"Swap one debt for another?"

"Matthew Thorne isn't going to come after you and beat you to a pulp," she pointed out. "Trust me, I just... I have this really good feeling about him. I just have to..."

For a moment, she thought back to the sight of the dead woman. The idea of ever seeing her again filled Stella with a sense of absolute dread, but at the same time she figured she could be brave for just long enough to talk to Matthew and try to persuade him to help. She might not even have to go back into the house.

"I can do it," she said firmly, through gritted teeth. "This might be a sign from the gods. A solution has fallen into our laps, and I for one am not going to just let it slip away."

"Stella -"

"And you can't stop me," she told him. "It's

my choice if I want to go up there and ask him. Even if I see her again, I can handle that."

"If you see *who* again?" he asked.

"It doesn't matter," she continued. "You'd only laugh if I told you. Besides, it'll be daytime, so it won't seem so bad." She paused, before taking a deep breath as she realized that she really had no other options. "I'm going to talk to Matthew Thorne, and I'm going to offer him anything he wants. And I don't care what he says, Gary, I'm going to get that money."

CHAPTER EIGHTEEN

"YOU DON'T HAVE TO do this," Gary said, watching as Stella finished checking her make-up. "The whole thing's crazy. That dude's never going to just hand over a load of money to you."

"Let me deal with that," she replied, still working on her lipstick. "You haven't met him, Gary. I have. He's different, there's something about him that..."

Her voice trailed off for a moment as she tried to work out how to explain. She knew that her plan sounded crazy, but at the same time she felt certain that there was a chance it might work. She'd sensed a connection with Matthew Thorne, something immediate that had drawn her to him, and she was sure he'd noticed it as well. Besides, she had no better ideas, and she was counting on her own ability to figure something out at the crucial time. No matter how bizarre the situation felt, she kept coming back to one immutable fact: Matthew Thorne was a decent man, she already knew that, and there had to be a way to get him to help.

"I can get the money from him," she said firmly. She was speaking as much to herself as to Gary now. "I know I can."

"I don't deserve you."

She glanced at him. In that moment, she remembered all the times her mother had begged her to end the relationship, telling her that Gary was no good, that he was a loser with no future; deep down, however, she felt that *she* was the lucky one. Nobody else in the whole world had ever made her feel the way Gary made her feel.

Alive.

Important.

Wanted.

"We're in this together," she replied, before making her way over. "There's only one thing I need from you, in exchange for me doing this." Reaching down, she put a hand on the side of his bruised face. "I need you to promise me, really promise from the bottom of your heart, that we're going to put this lifestyle behind us. Once we're free from Cole, and once we're out of Nice, we have to start living honestly, like normal people. Promise me that."

"Babe, you know that's what I want," he told her. "It's what I've always wanted."

"So you promise?"

"A million times over. A billion times."

"Once is enough," she replied, "so long as you stick to it."

"We're going to go somewhere amazing," he explained, placing a hand on the side of her waist. "How about Venice? Or Rome? Or Madrid? How about Monaco, we could -"

"How about somewhere a little quieter," she suggested, interrupting him. "I don't want to live in the fast lane, not after this. I want a quiet life, and a job working somewhere safe like a cafe, and I want us to just be normal people for a while. No massive plans, no attempts to get rich quick, no scams or schemes or dealings with shady characters. Just you, me, and the rest of our life. How does that sound?"

"Heaven," he said, looking up at her with a smile. "Who could ask for anything better than that?"

He paused, before putting a hand on her belly.

"And who knows?" he added. "Give it a year or two, and we might even be able to start popping out little Gary and little Stella."

"Let's take things one step at a time," she replied, gently moving his hand away. "I should get going. I've already called Matthew Thorne's office and arranged to meet him at six, and he likes people to show up at the right time."

"Is he sending another car to take you to his place?"

"I'm not going to his house," she explained, as a shudder passed through her chest. The idea of going to that house again filled her with dread. "I've arranged to see him at a restaurant in one of his favorite hotels in town."

***

Piano music drifted across the foyer as Stella sat near the reception desk and watched the clock. She'd been waiting for fifteen minutes, and to her surprise Matthew Thorne was now almost five minutes late. She knew that he was a stickler for punctuality, so she was starting to worry that he might have had second thoughts about meeting her at all.

Checking her phone, she saw that she still had no messages.

"Where are you?" she whispered, looking over at the door again, while trying to tell herself that it was too soon to worry.

Even the great Matthew Thorne was allowed to be late once in a while.

Suddenly her phone began to ring, but she

felt a flicker of disappointment as she looked down and saw Gary's name flashing on the screen. She briefly considered not answering, but finally she tapped to accept the call.

"I really can't talk right now," she said firmly.

"Are you with him yet?"

"Obviously not, or I wouldn't be answering the phone, would I?"

"Do you think he's going to show up?"

"Of course he is," she replied, although she couldn't help but notice a trace of uncertainty in her voice. She looked at the door again, and she was starting to wonder whether somehow there'd been a major communication mix-up. "Listen, if you -"

"What kind of car does he drive?"

"Why does that matter?"

"I'm just curious. Is he one of those rich assholes who drive around in a big limousine?"

"He has a limousine, yes, but -"

"I bet it's black and got tinted windows, all that shit."

"The guy's got money," she replied tersely, annoyed by Gary's constant questions, "and I suppose he values his privacy. That doesn't make him an asshole, it just makes him..."

Secretive?

Shy?

Suspicious?

She struggled for a moment to find the right word, preferably one that Gary wouldn't be able to twist into something negative.

"Confident," she managed finally, and at that particular moment she couldn't help but wish that Gary might take on a few of Matthew Thorne's more admirable traits. "He knows what he wants and what he likes, and he gets it. I actually think that's pretty cool."

"Alright, there's no need to start swooning over the bastard. I'm sure he farts and burps like any man. It's not like the sun shines out his backside or anything."

"I should go," she replied, mildly disgusted by her boyfriend. "I really don't want him to see me talking on the phone when he gets here. That wouldn't be very... elegant."

"Listen to you," Gary said with a chuckle, "fancying yourself as some kind of -"

Cutting the call before he had a chance to say anything else irritating, Stella switched her phone to silent and then slipped it into her purse. Taking out her compact, she checked her make-up and saw that it was all still in place, and then – hearing footsteps nearby – she looked up just as Matthew Thorne stumbled into the reception area.

Puzzled, she realized immediately that something was wrong. Whereas before Matthew had always seemed calm and collected, now he looked positively dazed, almost disheveled, as he turned and looked around the foyer. He seemed almost to not know where he was, and when he finally spotted Stella he didn't immediately react. Instead he stared at her for a few seconds as if he didn't even recognize her, before taking a moment to adjust his tie before making his way over.

Getting to her feet, Stella reminded herself that she had to seem elegant and sophisticated right from the start of the meeting.

"Good evening," she said with a faint smile, and she just managed in time to stop herself mentioning his tardiness. "I'm really glad you were able to see me at such short notice. I hope it wasn't too inconvenient."

"It's fine," he replied, clearly still flustered as he adjusted his tie again. "Believe it or not, I was expecting your call."

"You were?"

"Call it intuition," he added, and now he seemed almost scared as he glanced around the foyer. "Call it whatever you like," he muttered, his eyes darting from one direction to the next as if he was looking for something specific. "It's taken me all this time to really understand, but now I do. Now it all makes sense."

Stella waited for him to continue, but he once again seemed to be slipping into a daze. She could tell that he had a lot on his mind, and she didn't want to be too pushy, but at the same time she felt that she shouldn't wait too long. She had to focus on what she really needed from the evening, so after a few more seconds she touched the side of his arm, only for him to let out a gasp and pull back.

"Sorry," she said, "I just... I was wondering, should we go through to dinner?"

"Dinner?" He swallowed hard. "Yes," he said finally, with all the enthusiasm of a man on his way to face a firing squad. "Yes, let's go to dinner. Why not? After all, isn't that what we're here for?"

CHAPTER NINETEEN

"I'VE BEEN WAITING A long time for tonight," Matthew said softly, before furrowing his brow for a moment. "Do you believe in fate?"

Somewhat taken aback by that question, Stella wasn't quite sure how to answer. Fortunately the waiter had arrived with the starters, so she was able to take a few seconds to consider her response. Still, those seconds drained away quickly enough, leaving her still without any kind of witty response.

"I really don't know," she said finally, once the waiter was gone and steam from the soup began to rise past her face. "I haven't thought about it that much. I suppose I feel like everyone has a chance to shape their own destiny."

"But what if they don't?" he asked, his voice tense with what seemed to be fear. "Or what if they do, but once they've made their choices, there's no going back? What if time doesn't work the way we think it does?"

"I'm not -"

"Put it another way," he continued, leaning forward slightly, conspicuously ignoring his bowl of soup. "What if we have all the freedom we could ever want, but we can't change things that have already happened?"

"I suppose that's just life," Stella suggested awkwardly, still struggling to understand exactly what was wrong. She'd dismissed the idea that Matthew might be on drugs, but something about him seemed so very different. "You make a choice, and then you have to deal with the consequences. Believe me, there are some things I'd like to change if I could."

"Yes, but what if..."

He paused, and then he sighed.

"This soup smells really nice," Stella said, hoping to shift the topic of conversation onto a lighter topic. "I've never really been into soup, but this is great. What was it again? Parsnip and -"

"What if you already knew the choices that you'd made?" Matthew asked, interrupting her. "What if you have to live through them again, except this time you couldn't change what you'd done before?"

"I've never really been into philosophy a

whole lot," she told him, and she was starting to feel stupid. She'd never paid a lot of attention at school, and she always felt inadequate whenever people talked about anything serious. "I just take things as they come, you know? I get on with my life and try not to overthink it too much."

"The day after my wife died, a butterfly landed on my desk," Matthew told her.

"Butterflies are cool."

"It was beautiful," he continued, "and I just sat and watched it for the longest time. It didn't fly away, it didn't seem to mind me at all. It just stayed there, right in the middle of the desk. Its wings were mostly blue, with a little black, and as I watched that butterfly I couldn't shake the feeling that it was watching me in return."

"It probably was," Stella agreed, with a nervous style. "I hope you don't mind, but I was hoping to talk to you about -"

"And I got to thinking," Matthew said, ignoring her, "about why that butterfly was there. What did it want? Why would it simply rest there on my desk, in my office, when it had a whole garden outside to explore? It had flown through the window and landed very deliberately, or at least that's the impression I got. The butterfly's presence was no accident. In that moment, I knew that the butterfly had arrived specifically to see me."

"Right," Stella said cautiously. "That

sounds... cool."

"And this was the day after my wife had died," Matthew added. "That seems important somehow."

"You must have been feeling awful."

"I started to wonder whether the butterfly was a sign," he explained. "I know this might sound far-fetched, but it was as if the butterfly was in some way returning to me, and I began to think that my wife..."

Stella waited for him to finish.

"You think your wife was reincarnated as a butterfly?" she suggested finally.

"It crawled across the desk and onto my hand," he told her, "and in that moment, I felt so very free and happy. I can't explain the sensation, except to say that the butterfly found some way to make me feel as though life was worth living. And Martha had told me, before she died, that she'd come back if she could and give me some kind of sign. At the time, I just assumed that she was rambling, but her words returned to me as the butterfly sat on my hand. And then it flew away, straight back out the window, as if it's work was done."

"That's really nice," Stella said, figuring that she at least had to let him finish the story.

"But then I started thinking about the life cycle of the butterfly," Matthew continued. "It made no sense. Martha had died just the day before, and obviously the butterfly – at least in its caterpillar form – must have existed for longer than that. So it couldn't have been Martha, could it? Because their lives couldn't... overlap like that, could they? There's just no logic in that, unless..."

Again, Stella waited for him to finish, but this time he seemed to be lost in thought. She was starting to think that her opportunity had arrived.

"I need to ask you something," she said finally. "Something important."

"I'm sure you do," he replied, fixing her with a firm stare. "I've been waiting for you to tell me why we're here tonight."

"The thing is..."

Suddenly feeling tongue-tied, Stella tried to work out how exactly to explain her predicament. She didn't want to simply ask for the cash, yet in effect she knew there was only so much she could do to dress up her words as anything more noble.

"It's complicated," she managed to say finally, "but the real problem is that I'm in trouble." She paused, watching his face as she tried to judge his reaction. "A lot of trouble, actually," she continued, "and time's running out and I don't have anywhere else to turn. You don't know me, you have no reason to help me or to care about what happens to me, but I -"

"You need money."

She instinctively wanted to deny that suggestion, but she knew she had to be honest.

"I wouldn't ask," she explained, barely able to meet his gaze, "if this wasn't a situation that's really about life or death. Believe me, I know how wrong this all is, and I know how I sound, but the truth is that I'm desperate and -"

"And you need a lot of money or your boyfriend will be killed," Matthew said suddenly, interrupting her. "He's involved with some gangsters and their patience has run out, and they're going to make an example of him if he doesn't hand over the money he owes by midnight tonight. They've already roughed him up, they could have killed him by now, but in desperation you're here to try to get the money by any means possible. You know he can't simply run away, you know you need every euro he owes, and you saw it sitting in my safe. That's pretty much the situation, right?"

Staring at him open-mouthed, Stella had no idea how he'd managed to figure out so much.

"Well, I -"

"So now we have to go to the house to *fetch* the money," Matthew said through gritted teeth. He seemed increasingly agitated, and after a moment Stella noticed that he was gripping the sides of the table. A moment after that, he got to his feet, nudging the table in the process. "That's the plan, isn't it?" he continued. "There's no way out, so we might as well just get it over and done with right now."

"I just -"

"There's no point delaying, is there?" he asked, his voice trembling slightly. Was it fear, or anger, or both? "There are no other possibilities. We both know what has to happen, so we should just get on with it."

"You don't *have* to help," she pointed out.

"Don't I?"

"Well, no," she replied, trying to figure out why he was reacting so strangely. "You can tell me to leave. You can swear at me and kick me out and call me all sorts of names."

"Would that change anything?"

"What do you want in return?"

"For the money?" He paused, fixing her with a glare that made her feel extremely uncomfortable. "I don't know that there's anything I can possibly ask for," he continued. "That ship has sailed, and now there's really nothing to do except let things unravel as they must."

"Right," Stella said cautiously, still not quite understanding the strange sense of doom that seemed to have filled every fiber of his being. "So does that mean..."

She paused, struggling to believe that her plan had really worked.

"Does that mean," she continued finally,

"that you're going to help us?"

"What choice do I have?" he asked. "There's no point delaying this for even a moment longer, Stella Ward. It's time for us to go back to the house." He paused for a moment, eyeing her with a curious gaze. "Are you ready?"

"The house?"

She swallowed hard.

"I... guess so," she said cautiously, even though she'd hoped to find some way to avoid ever setting foot in the place again. Still, she knew she couldn't exactly argue.

"This way," he replied, as he led her away from the table. "Do you know the strange thing? I was once told that these things come in threes, but that's the only part I've never been able to work out. There's you, and there's me, so where's the third of us?"

"I'm not sure what you mean."

"Forget it," he said. "I'm rambling. So, tell me... do you ever get the feeling that you've arrived late, at the end of somebody else's story?"

CHAPTER TWENTY

AS THE IRON GATES swung open, Matthew Thorne's car drove through and stopped at the edge of the driveway. A moment later the doors opened, and Matthew and Stella stepped out. Once they were clear of the car, the vehicle reversed and the gates swung shut with a loud, heavy jolt.

***

"I can't even begin to tell you how much this means," Stella said a couple of minutes later, as she and Matthew walked into the house. "We'll pay you back, I swear, it just... I suppose it'll just take time."

"Time's one thing we don't really have," Matthew replied, stopping under the chandelier and turning to her. He hesitated for a few seconds, and then he began to look around the room. "I don't remember," he added. "Why is it so difficult to keep everything in order?"

Although she wanted to ask Matthew what he meant, Stella wasn't sure that she'd actually get much of an answer. She told herself that she simply had to focus on the task of getting the money and then getting that to Gary, so she stayed silent as Matthew continued to look around the room. As she looked around, she tried to remember that she wouldn't have to stay for long.

Suddenly a slamming sound rang out from upstairs.

Stella looked up toward the landing, and then she turned to see that Matthew was watching her.

"You heard that," he said stiffly. "I can see it in your eyes."

"It might have been the wind," she suggested, even though she knew that the explanation wouldn't carry much weight. "Or the house... settling..."

"You saw something when you were here before, didn't you?" he asked. "I know she's here, but she never lets me see her. Tell me, is she still beautiful?"

"I don't know what you -"

"Don't lie," he said firmly. "Not now, of all times. This is the price I ask, in exchange for the money. Tell me that she's still beautiful."

Stella swallowed hard.

"I don't know what you mean," she said, unable to actually acknowledge the existence of something paranormal. After a moment, she checked her watch.

"Forget it," Matthew told her, turning and making his way to the stairs. "I shouldn't have asked. I'll get the money."

"Wait," Stella said, "I -"

"Stay right there," he added, quickly heading through to one of the other rooms. He mumbled something else under his breath, but the words were lost as his echoing footsteps disappeared into the distance.

Reaching into her bag, Stella took out her phone and saw several more missed calls from Gary. Since the phone had been on silent, none of those calls had made a sound, but now she felt as if she needed to give him at least a small update. A sliver of hope. She glanced toward the doorway to make sure that Matthew wasn't about to return, and then she quickly unlocked the phone and began to type a message:

All good. Soon done. :)

She saw immediately that the message had been read, but she wasn't ready to get into a long conversation so she slipped her phone away and then looked again toward the doorway. She couldn't hear Matthew anywhere in the house, but she told herself that was a good thing; it meant he wasn't talking to himself again, or on the verge of a breakdown, and she tried to focus on the fact that she simply needed to get the money and leave. Her second visit to the house would certainly be her last. After a moment, however, she heard some of Matthew Thorne's words from earlier ringing in her ears.

"So tell me," he'd said as they'd left the restaurant, "do you ever get the feeling that you've arrived late, at the end of somebody else's story?"

She hadn't been sure at the time what he'd meant, and she wasn't sure now, but she couldn't help wondering whether she should have explained the situation a little more clearly. Sure, he was giving her the money, but she could understand how he might feel as if he was arriving 'late' to everything that had been happening in her life. Did she owe it to him to sit him down and explain the entire situation with Cole in detail? She figured the time for that would come later, when she eventually returned to repay every euro and every cent, and she *would* return to make good on the debt. That much, she knew for certain. Perhaps not to the house itself, but she'd arrange to meet him and she'd tell him the whole story.

After a moment, realizing that Matthew seemed to be taking a very long time, she began to make her way over to the doorway.

Looking through into the next room, she immediately saw him kneeling in front of the safe. He'd placed a pile of cash in a bag on the floor, but now he seemed somehow frozen in place. Her eyes were immediately drawn to the safe's interior, and she saw that there must be millions of euros sitting on the shelves. For a few seconds, she couldn't help but imagine what she could do with so much money, but she quickly reminded herself that she should just be grateful for any help at all.

Suddenly Matthew turned and looked directly at her.

"Hi," Stella said, annoyed with herself for having been spotted. "Sorry, I didn't mean to snoop, I just... came to see if I could help with anything."

"If you could *help* with anything?" he replied through gritted teeth.

"Yeah," she said, and now she was worried that she might have upset him, and that he might change his mind about helping, and that she might have snatched defeat from the jaws of victory. "I shouldn't have done, though. I'll just go and wait in the hall."

"Do you recognize this room?" he asked.

"Recognize it?"

"Do you recognize any of it?" he continued,

picking up the bag of money and then slowly getting to his feet. "Do you recognize *me*?"

"I don't know what you mean," she told him awkwardly.

"It's okay," he said, as he began to make his way toward her, "I didn't really think that you would. I'm just trying to make sense of this madness, but in truth I rather think that's beyond me. I've had a long time to try to get my head around everything, and I've failed. The human mind is a magnificent thing, it helps us in so many ways, but I doubt it can do much when presented with matters of the cosmos. I should have made that woman at the fairground explain more, but I didn't really take her seriously at the time."

As he reached Stella, he stopped and looked deep into her eyes. Although she wanted to turn away, she knew she had to be patient. And polite.

"Trying to figure that sort of thing out," Matthew continued, "can really drive a man crazy, don't you think?"

"I wouldn't know," she said, trying to be diplomatic.

"Believe me, I've given it a great deal of thought," he told her, "and I have a feeling that you will too, one day. When you're far from here, so far away that you won't even understand how you traveled such a distance. Even now, standing here and knowing what I know, I can literally feel my mind straining against its limits. I can feel my own failure to comprehend. I suppose I really just have to let it all happen now. Now that I've reached..."

He paused, before holding the bag out toward her.

"The end," he added.

She waited, but he seemed to be finished. Cautiously, she reached out and took the bag; she felt him hold the handle firmly for a few seconds, but he finally released his grip and the bag was hers.

"Thanks," she told him, and at that moment she spotted – for the first time – a large metal sculpture on the far wall, depicting what appeared to be a snake eating its own tail.

"Do you like that?" Matthew asked.

She turned to him, somewhat startled.

"I only just noticed it," she told him. She wanted to leave, but she knew she shouldn't be rude. "There's just -"

Before she could finish, something heavy bumped against the floor of the room directly above. Shocked, Bella stepped back, brushing against the wall as she looked up at the ceiling. Her heart was racing, and this time she had to really force herself to stand her ground instead of racing out of the house with the bag of money.

"She tried to understand," Matthew whispered.

"Who are you talking about?" Stella asked.

He opened his mouth, as if to reply, but then he hesitated for a few seconds before grabbing her by the arm and forcing her out into the hallway.

"It doesn't matter," he told her as he led her toward the front. "I suppose nothing does, not anymore. You've got your money. That's all you really want, isn't it?"

"No, I -"

"So you should be grateful for that," he added, opening the door and shoving her out toward the top of the steps with surprising abruptness. "You've got everything you could have ever wanted, and you should enjoy it."

She turned to him.

"While you still can," he said. "Promise me one thing, though. Really promise."

"Anything," she stammered.

"Don't ever come back," he continued. "It'll be hard, but just try, for my sake. Promise me that you'll do everything in your power to never, ever come back here."

"But -"

"Promise me!" he snarled.

Just as she was about to tell him that she'd be back to repay him when she could, and that she was enormously grateful, Stella saw a figure standing on the main staircase. She stared for a moment at the ghostly figure of Martha Thorne, before Matthew slammed the door shut with such force that she felt a rush of air and took an instinctive step back.

"Thank you," she stammered, horrified by what she'd just seen. "I'll try."

After a moment, realizing that Matthew clearly had no interest in talking to her any further, she looked down at the bag. She carefully pulled it open, and she let out an involuntary gasp as she she huge wads of cash. Even without counting methodically, she could tell that there had to be at least fifty thousand euros in the bag, probably a lot more, and finally she took a step back.

Looking at the front door, she realized that whatever madness had gripped Matthew Thorne was none of her business. Sure, she'd repay the money eventually, but Matthew was clearly going through some kind of insanity that could only be dealt with by professionals. She wished him well, yet at the same time she knew she had her own life to live, so after a moment she turned and began to make her way down the steps at the front of the house.

The time had come to find Gary, pay Cole, and get the hell out of Nice forever.

CHAPTER TWENTY-ONE

AS HER FOOTSTEPS CRUNCHED across the gravel driveway, Stella made her way through the darkness and saw the large iron gate ahead. Just as she was starting to wonder whether she'd have to climb over the wall again, the gate began to creak open, and she stopped for a moment to look back toward the house.

She watched the windows. There was no sign of Matthew, but she figured that he must have activated the gate in order to let her leave. For a moment, she heard his voice echoing in her thoughts:

"Don't ever come back," he'd said firmly. "It'll be hard, but just try, for my sake. Promise me that you'll do everything in your power to never, ever come back here."

And then he'd briefly erupted in a flash of anger:

"Promise me!"

"I'll get the money back to you," she whispered in the cold night air. "I don't know how or when, but I'll do the right thing eventually."

She wanted to go and bang on the door, to tell him to his face that she'd make amends, but she reminded herself that she'd already promised to heed his warning. When the day eventually arrived, she'd just have to find some other way to get the money to him.

Turning, she saw the lights of Nice in the distance and realized that she faced yet another long walk back to town, but this time she didn't mind too much. She had the money, and she figured that within twenty-four hours she and Gary would be far away.

With a faint smile, she began to make her way out past the open gate.

"Hey!"

Startled, she saw a figure step in front of her, and it took a moment before she realized that she was looking directly at Gary.

"What are you doing here?" she asked.

"Is a man not allowed to worry about his girl?" he replied, putting his hands on the sides of her arms before looking down at the bag. "Did you get it?"

"Yes, I -"

"You're a bloody miracle-worker!" he said, leaning close and kissing her on the cheek, then giving her a second, bigger kiss.

Although she struggled for a moment, she had to surrender as Gary forced his tongue into her mouth. The kiss was much more forceful than usual, and at first she couldn't quite work out why he was acting so strangely, until she suddenly became aware of footsteps approaching. She tried to pull away, only for Gary to intensify the kiss, but in that moment somebody walked past and brushed against her shoulder.

"Wait!" Stella gasped finally, managing to pull away and turn to the two other men, who were already walking toward Matthew Thorne's house. "What's happening?"

"Just chill," Gary said, lowering his voice to a conspiratorial hiss. "Babe, there's more than one way to skin a cat, right? Just like there's more than one way to pay a debt."

"What are you talking about?" she asked, as she began to realize that yet again Gary had sprung a surprise.

"So this is the place, huh?" a voice said, as one of the other men turned to them. "Exactly how much did you say was in the safe?"

"There's loads in there," Gary replied, before Stella could say a word. "She reckons there's millions just sitting around, waiting to be taken. Seriously, Cole, I wasn't lying when I promised you the biggest payday of your life. You can walk out of here with enough money to go anywhere! Dude, isn't this what we always dreamed of?"

"You sold Matthew Thorne out to Cole?" Stella said, turning to Gary with a genuine sense of disbelief. "I told you about the safe because -"

"Because you wanted to make everything right," Gary said. "You thought that meant running away like scared little rats, but think of the bigger picture." He leaned closer and whispered into her ear. "This haul means Cole's going to trust me. It means we can stick around and he'll give us the biggest business opportunities. Plus, we get to keep some of the stash. Babe, we don't have to leave Nice, we can stay and work for Cole properly."

Horrified, Stella tried to tell herself that she was misunderstanding what he'd just suggested.

"We're made for life," he continued. "Tonight, we're going from the bottom of the food chain to the -"

Suddenly, unable to stop herself, Stella slapped him hard on the side of the face.

"Looks like someone's in a spot of trouble," Cole chuckled, just as the metal gates began to creak shut. "Gary, my friend, you need to be the master of your own castle."

"We have to leave!" Stella told Gary firmly,

before turning to Cole and the other man. "You both have to leave too! You have no right to be here!"

"Calm down," the other man said, stepping forward until his features were visible in the moonlight.

At that moment, Stella recognized him as Cole's friend Walter.

"Don't cause trouble," Gary whispered, grabbing Stella by the arm.

"Yeah, don't cause trouble," Walter continued with a grin. "You should be pleased. This time a few hours ago, your boyfriend was a guaranteed stiff. He's really pulled himself out of the fire here."

"*If* what he said turns out to be true," Cole added, keeping his eyes fixed firmly on Stella. "M'am, what's the security like at this place? Gary says it's pretty minimal, but I feel as if you have a better handle on things."

"I'm not helping you," she told him, before stepping closer and shoving the bag of money into his hands. "This is what you wanted! It's every cent that we owe you and more, so take it! There's nothing else here for you! This is private property and Matthew won't want you here, so you have to leave!" She waited for Cole to take the money; she shoved it into his chest again, but this seemed to provoke only amusement. "This is the fifty thousand!" she snapped. "Take it!"

"Gary makes it sound like this place is completely unguarded," Cole replied, smiling down at her, "with just one rich guy in a big old house, and a nice full safe waiting for us to take a little look. So, really, I don't have very much interest in a *mere* fifty thousand euros when I can walk away with millions in cash." He paused, before reaching up and placing a finger on one side of Stella's face. "You can keep the money."

She instantly pulled away.

"Did you hear that?" Gary said excitedly, rushing to Stella's side. "It's all ours! This is bigger than our wildest dreams!"

"We're not staying here and working for you," Stella sneered, looking up at Cole. "We don't want anything to do with you!"

"She doesn't mean that," Gary said hurriedly. "Don't listen to her, she's just getting emotional. She does that sometimes."

"Are you kidding?" Stella replied, letting go of the bag of money, which dropped to the floor. As she turned to Gary, she realized that everything he'd been saying for days was now out the window. "You want to stay here and still work with this creep?"

"Just maybe cut the language down a little," Gary said, wincing slightly. "There's no need to be rude."

"You're sick!" she snapped angrily, shoving him hard in the chest. "You're a liar!"

"Calm down!" he hissed, trying to grab her wrists to hold her still. "You're embarrassing me!"

"I never should have trusted you!" she shouted, pushing him again. "I should have listened to everyone who told me you're just a criminal piece of trash! I can't believe I actually thought you might be a good person!"

"Babe..."

"I don't think your girlfriend likes you very much," Cole suggested with a smile. "You're not going to let her talk to you like that, are you?"

"Babe, please," Gary whispered, putting his hands on her waist, "you don't understand how it works with these people. You're making me look weak."

"You're making yourself look like a lying asshole!" she snapped.

"Stella -"

"I don't want anything to do with you ever again!" she yelled, as tears began to run down her face. "I'm leaving! I'm going back to England and I hope you rot in hell!"

"Don't make me do this," Gary fumed. "You're putting me in a very awkward situation."

"I don't care what you do!" she shouted, shoving him again. "You can keep your dirty stinking money and -"

Suddenly Gary slapped her hard, hitting her on the side of the face with such force that she stepped back. Startled, with a stinging pain on her cheek, she tripped and fell, landing hard on the ground. Shocked by what had just happened, she stared up at Gary and saw the pained expression on his face.

"I didn't want to do that," he told her, "but you really left me no choice."

"I..."

Her voice trailed off. After a moment, hearing laughter, she turned to Cole, but at that moment she spotted a sliver of light in the distance. Looking toward the house, she was horrified to see that the front door was open and that Matthew Thorne was standing silhouetted against the bright hallway. In that instant, she felt a sickening sense of dread in the pit of her stomach as she realized that the situation was rapidly snowballing out of control.

"No," she whispered, staring at Matthew's silhouetted figure. "Please..."

"Hello!" Walter called out, hurrying toward the steps, waving at Matthew. "There's no need to be alarmed! Sir, we're just here to perform a little security check, that's all!" He hurried up the steps. "It's all good, man! There's no need to freak out, we're all friends here!"

"No," Stella said, slowly getting to her feet. "Matthew!" she called out. "Don't listen to these people! Shut the door! Lock it and call the police! Don't let them -"

In a flash, Walter punched Matthew hard in the face, sending him crumpling to the ground with a loud cracking sound.

"No!" Stella screamed, stumbling forward, only for Cole to shove her back toward Gary.

"We're going in," Cole said firmly, "and you're coming with us. I want to know exactly how to get into that safe. Hopefully Mr. Thorne is smart enough to give us exactly what we want, but in case he's not..." He paused for a moment, clearly struggling to contain a laugh. "Well, Stella, that's where you might prove very useful."

CHAPTER TWENTY-TWO

"JUST STAY CALM," GARY whispered a few minutes later, as he and Stella followed the others into the house. "This really doesn't have to end badly. Cole's not a violent man."

She turned to him.

"Only when he's pushed," he added, still clutching the bag of money that he'd picked up out on the driveway. "If this Thorne guy's smart, he'll open the safe and no-one has to get hurt."

"I hate you," she said through gritted teeth.

"You've told me that before."

"I really mean it this time," she continued, and she was certain that something was different now. "You don't even know *how* to tell the truth, do you? You just lie to get whatever you want, and you don't care who you hurt in the process."

"Babe," he said, touching her arm, "you're just -"

"Leave me alone!" she snapped angrily, pulling away. "If Matthew Thorne gets hurt, I'll make sure you pay."

"You don't mean that," he told her. "You always get angry at me, but you always remember how much you love me in the end. And I love you back, Stella. We're made for each other, we're like Romeo and Juliet, and that's not ever going to change. I'll provide for you, Stella, I promise. I'm your man."

"You're nothing but filth and -"

Before she could finish, Stella heard the sound of glass smashing. Turning, she looked toward the far side of the hallway, and a moment later she realized she could hear a scuffle breaking out.

"Leave him alone!" she called out, rushing to the doorway. "What are you doing to -"

Suddenly she saw that Matthew was on his knees in front of the closed safe, trying to slice his own wrists open when a large piece of glass. Walter, meanwhile, was desperately trying to pull him back, while Cole finally stepped around and wrenched the glass from his hand.

"There's no need to react like that," Cole said firmly, as Matthew tried desperately to grab some more broken glass from the floor. "My friend, your situation is better than you realize."

He watched Matthew for a moment longer, before turning to Stella.

"He smashed that vase and tried to cut his own wrists open," he explained. "Can you believe that? All I did was ask him very nicely if he'd mind opening the safe, and he reacted by trying to top himself. Is this guy a little short in the brains department?"

Although she found it hard to believe what Cole had just said, Stella couldn't help but watch as Matthew tried again and again to reach for some more glass. She told herself that he was merely trying to defend himself, but after a moment Matthew took a large shard and tried to plunge it into his wrists. Only a moment of quick thinking by Walter prevented that, and soon Matthew was being pulled back kicking and screaming toward the safe.

"Is he right in the head?" Gary asked, stepping up behind Stella. "He doesn't seem it."

"He's complicated," she replied, watching as Matthew tried over and over to break free. "You're invading his home. What do you expect him to do, roll out the red carpet?"

Letting out a grunt, Walter finally managed to subdue Matthew and throw him against the wall. Although Matthew briefly tried to get back up, Walter kicked him hard in the chest and sent him crumpling down, this time for good. Stepping away,

Walter gathered up the glass and set it aside, and he was noticeably out of breath as he made his way over to join Cole at the safe.

"Can you break into this thing?" Cole asked.

"Just get the combination from this Thorne guy," Walter suggested.

"He's being stubborn so far," Cole replied. "If you can break into it, that'd be easier. Otherwise I'm going to have to get creative with my ways to drag the information out of him."

Spotting Matthew starting to crawl over to the glass, Stella rushed forward and dropped to her knees.

"Hey, don't do that," she said to him, gently pushing him back. "You don't need to. I'm so sorry that they followed me here, I swear I didn't know that any of this was going to happen, but no-one has to get hurt."

"I begged you not to come back!" he sneered.

"If you just do what they want, they'll leave!" she said firmly.

"That's right," Cole said with a smile. "Persuade your friend to cooperate, and we can be out of here in ten minutes flat."

"I can't go through with it," Matthew said through gritted teeth, looking toward the glass. "I want the end now, I don't want to let it all happen again. Why can't I at least control this one last thing?"

"These people are dangerous," Stella told him. "I'm sorry, but that's just the truth. They're *really* dangerous, and they'll hurt you if you don't give them what they want. I think it'd be better if you accept that now."

"I don't need you to tell me who or what they are," Matthew replied, turning to her. "Trust me, I know far more than you do."

"Let's wait outside," Gary said, stepping up behind Stella and grabbing her arm, then attempting to pull her toward the door. "We don't need to be in here, let's just let the guys handle the situation in their own way."

"Everything's going to be okay," Stella said, ignoring Gary and trying once again to get through to Matthew. "There's no need to -"

Suddenly feeling Gary pulling on her arm, she turned and pushed him back.

"Don't touch me!" she snapped angrily.

"You're causing trouble," he replied with a heavy sigh.

"Just leave me alone," she told him, unable to hide the sense of pure disgust that she felt as she looked at his face. "Why can't you get it through your thick head that I don't want anything to do with you ever again?"

"It's over," Matthew said, leaning back against the wall and putting his head in his hands.

"Nothing's over," Stella explained, heading back over to him.

"You don't get it," he replied, looking at her with a horrified expression on his face. "You will do, one day. You'll understand it all, but it'll be far too late."

Reaching out, he grabbed her by the wrist.

"By the time you realize," he added, "you won't be able to stop any of it."

"So what's the deal with this safe?" Cole asked, making his way over and stopping next to them both. "My man here says he can get it open, but he reckons it'll take a couple of hours. The way I see it, it'd be much easier if we had a nice, cooperative gentleman who's willing to just give us the code." He nudged Matthew with his boot. "How about it? Are you going to be that nice, cooperative gentleman?"

"You have no choice," Matthew replied, staring up at him.

"Come again?" Cole asked.

"You think you do, but you don't," Matthew continued, and now his voice was trembling with fear. "You think you're in charge, but you're on rails. Every choice you think you need to make, has already been made. Even your anger has already been set. You don't see it, you can't *possibly* see it, but you're already doomed."

"Is that right?" Cole asked with a grin. "You

seem pretty confident, for a man who just tried to gash his own arms open."

"That's because I've seen it," Matthew told him. "It's because I know everything you don't know."

"I don't like people acting smarter than me," Cole replied. "You've rubbed me up the wrong way, my friend, and I'm afraid you're going to regret that. Now, I'll give you one last chance to do the smart thing, but it really *will* be your last chance." He crouched down. "Give me the combination to the safe."

He waited, but Matthew simply stared at him.

"Is he stupid?" Cole asked, turning to Stella. "That happens with these rich bastards sometimes, doesn't it? Their brains just don't quite work."

Before Stella could reply, she heard a loud banging sound and turned to see that Walter was already trying to smash his way into the safe.

"That won't work," Matthew said under his breath, watching Walter with what seemed to be a hint of glee. "He can hit it for the rest of his life, but he'll barely make a dent. The only way into that safe is with the right code."

"So how about you *give* us the code?" Cole asked.

"I will," Matthew replied, turning to him, "but not yet. It's too soon. I'll give it to you when the time is right. Or will I? I'm really not sure."

"Is that so?" Cole said with a faint smile, as the banging sound became louder and louder. "Well, I hope you'll forgive me for trying to hurry that moment along a little."

He paused, and then he launched into a flurry of punches, hitting Matthew in the face over and over. Stella screamed and tried to pull him away, but – as the sound of Walter smashing the safe continued – she felt blood splattering against her face as Cole tore into Matthew with increasing ferocity. At the same time, somehow, Matthew was laughing.

CHAPTER TWENTY-THREE

"WHAT ARE YOU DOING?" Stella asked a few minutes later, once she and Matthew had been locked together in the office. "Why don't you just give them the code?"

In the distance, a steady thumping sound indicated that Walter was still trying to use brute force to get into the safe.

"You don't understand," Matthew whispered, slurring his words. His face was bloodied and battered, and he could barely sit up Stella tried her best to tend to his wounds. "It's not time. Not yet. He might be able to force the safe open, if he can figure out its weak points. I just don't quite remember."

"These people aren't messing around," she told him. "Gary's worked with them before, and they're killers. Just last year a guy washed up near the port, and everyone knows Cole was the one who'd had him murdered. Matthew, all the money in that safe isn't worth risking your life for."

"It's not about that," he said, barely managing to look up at her. "It's about things happening the way they're supposed to happen. From the moment I saw you in that restaurant, I've known..."

His voice trailed off for a few seconds.

Stella dabbed at a wound on the side of his head, trying to wipe away as much blood as possible.

"I've known how this has to play out," Matthew continued. "Nothing can be delayed, I've learned that much over the years. Nothing can be changed. And nothing can be hurried, either. I just wish I knew which one's the third version."

"You make it sound like you have no choice."

"You'll realize eventually," he told her. "Everything has to be... in its right place."

She opened her mouth to reply, but she was starting to think that he might be delirious. Not just from the beating he'd endured at Cole's hands, but from everything that had happened in his life. She only knew the basics, but it was clear to her now that Matthew Thorne's grip on reality wasn't entirely firm. She wiped some more blood from his cheek and then, getting to her feet, she made her way over to the only window in the room.

"You can't break out," Matthew told her.

"You can't stop me trying," she replied, although she instantly felt that the window was firmly secured. "Where are the keys?"

"The windows have been locked for years."

"Yes, but there must be keys!"

"I don't -"

"Just tell me where they are!" she shouted, filled with frustration as she turned to him.

"In a bowl in the kitchen."

"Why are they in a bowl in the kitchen?"

"That's where Martha used to put them," he explained groggily. "I thought about moving them, but then I realized... that's where they've always been. That's where I remember them being the first time, so I can't change anything."

"There has to be a phone," she said, hurrying to the desk.

"There's no phone in here."

"It's an office!"

"There wasn't a phone before," he replied, "so I couldn't put one in now because -"

"I get it," she snapped, "there wasn't one before. Whatever that means." Sighing, she stopped for a moment and looked around the room. She felt certain that there had to be a way out, if only she could be smart enough to come up with a plan.

Far off in another part of the house, the rhythmic banging sound continued as Walter, Cole and Gary tried to get into the safe.

Hurrying back around the desk, Stella headed to the door and tried to pull it open. She could tell that something was wedging the handles shut from the other side; Gary had told her that he was sealing her away for her own protection, but she told herself that he wasn't exactly the most practical guy in the world. Dropping to her knees, she tried to peer through the keyhole and figure out how he'd secured the door, since she figured that it should be possible to undo his work. After a few seconds, however, she realized that for once he seemed to have done a good job.

Behind her, Matthew began to chuckle.

"What's so funny?" she asked, turning to him.

She waited, but he simply continued laughing.

"You don't seem to be taking this very seriously," she said firmly.

"On the contrary," he replied, "I'm taking it as seriously as anyone can take anything. It's just that I know there's nothing we can do to change what's going to happen. So why not be a little light-hearted in these moments?"

"Rubbish," she said, getting to her feet and grabbing the chair from behind the desk, then hurrying to the window. "You might be willing to give up, but I'm not. I'm getting us out of here!"

With that, she swung the chair at the glass. The chair quickly rebounded, however, and the same thing happened when she tried again.

"It's toughened," Matthew explained, sitting up slightly. "It was like that when I moved in."

"So there's really no way for us to get out?" she asked, feeling a sliver of hopelessness in her chest.

"Sometimes you just have to accept your fate," he told her. "Sometimes there's just no way to change anything, no matter how hard you try."

"I don't believe that," she replied. "I grew up dirt poor. My mum raised five kids on her own after my dad died young, and she used to tell me that I'd never amount to anything. My four sisters listened to her, they let her batter them down, but I refused. I always knew that I had a future, so I got out of town as soon as I could. I didn't even care where I was going, but I knew I wasn't going to spend the rest of my life in Dover. I'm still not where I want to be, but at least I know I have a choice. At least I know it's in my hands. And that's why I won't give up and just sit here like an idiot."

"You think we can change anything?" he asked with a faint smile. "Okay, fine, let's give it a shot. Let's try to change something right now."

Before Stella could reply, Matthew turned

and looked at the wall, and a moment later he slammed his forehead against the edge of the fireplace. Letting out a loud scream, he did the same thing over and over, until Stella reached him and began to pull him away.

Laughing manically, Matthew slipped free and bashed his head again, this time cracking open a cut just above his left eye. This time Stella managed to pull him away and drag him across the room, but he was still laughing loudly as blood gushed from the wound.

"You're insane!" she stammered, setting him down on the floor and then straddling him as she tried to examine the injury. "Were you trying to kill yourself?"

"You said we can change things," he chuckled, twisting wildly in an attempt to get free. "I was only testing to see whether you're right!"

"Let me see that," she replied, trying to hold his head still as more and more blood ran down onto the carpet. "I think you've broken something!"

"No!" he shouted, reaching up and putting his bloodied hands on the sides of her face. "Nothing's broken! Don't you see? That's the whole point, it *can't* be broken! Even this was always supposed to happen! I'd forgotten about it until now, but I remember!"

"You're completely delirious," she said, still trying to hold him still. "You belong in a -"

She caught herself just in time, although in truth she was more and more convinced that Matthew Thorne's problems ran deep. Previously, she'd assumed that he was simply a little off-kilter, but now she could tell that he'd completely lost his mind. He didn't seem to care as blood burst from the wound above his eye; if anything, his laughter was getting louder, as if he was enjoying himself, and she realized now that she couldn't do anything to help him. She could try to keep him alive, but he needed to be seen by actual professionals.

"I don't know what happened to make you this way," she told him, "but I'll do what I can to help you. Can you even hear me? I'll do whatever I can to get you fixed up."

She waited, but he was still laughing, and she realized that he hadn't heard a word.

Suddenly she heard a scratching sound at the door. Looking across the room, she realized that the banging sound in the distance had stopped, and a moment later the door swung open to reveal Gary and Walter.

"He needs a doctor," she told them, her voice trembling with rage.

"He's going to need more than that," Gary replied. "Walter managed to get the safe open."

"I work miracles," Walter said with a grin.

"Cole wants you both back through there," Gary continued. "He's got what he wants, but he's not happy that he had to do it the hard way. I'm sorry, I've tried to talk some sense into him, but he *really* doesn't like it when he feels he's been disrespected."

"It's okay!" Matthew said, grinning from ear to bloody ear as he looked up at Stella. "We can still change things, right? That's what you told me! There's no need to worry, because we can change everything! It doesn't have to happen like this! You told me!"

As Gary and Walter made their way closer, Stella could only look down at Matthew as his laughter became stronger and stronger, and as his entire body began to shake.

CHAPTER TWENTY-FOUR

"THERE MUST BE MILLIONS in here," Cole said calmly as he took the last wad of money out of the safe. "My conservative estimate is... three million euros. That's a lot of money to keep sitting around for a rainy day."

He turned and looked over his shoulder, to where Stella and Matthew had been forced to kneel in the middle of the room.

"Not that I'm complaining, of course," he added, tossing the money onto the pile and then getting to his feet. "It'll take time to feed three million into the system, but I've got a lot of experience. By the time I'm done with all of this, I'll be able to afford to retire." He walked over to Stella and looked down at her. "Not that I *will* retire, of course," he said with a grin, "because I really enjoy my job."

He tried to touch one side of her face.

She turned away.

Grinning, he touched her other cheek.

She instantly spat at him.

"We're going to work with Cole," Gary said eagerly from the other side of the room. "You and me, Stella. We're going to be sorted for life."

She turned to him.

"You're disgusting," she sneered.

"You'll calm down," he told her.

"Don't count on it!"

"I'm not going to bother asking why so much money was in that safe," Cole said, stepping over to Matthew. "It's probably pocket change to a man like you, isn't it?"

"It had to be there," Matthew replied, looking up at him as blood ran down his face. "It just... had to, that's all."

"Is that right?" Cole asked.

"Don't hurt him!" Stella said firmly. "Don't you dare do anything else to him!"

"Get her out of here," Cole muttered, keeping his gaze fixed firmly on Matthew. "She's starting to irritate me."

Stella got to her feet, but at that moment Gary hurried up behind her and grabbed her arms. Although she tried to struggle, she was powerless as he pulled her back toward the edge of the room.

"Let go of me!" she hissed.

"We'll talk about this later, yeah?" Gary said, before kissing the side of her neck.

"Don't touch me!" she screamed, but again she was unable to break free.

"I like it when you're spicy," Gary told her. "That's always been the key to you and me, hasn't it? We're so good at fighting! And at making up after..."

"My time is very valuable," Cole said, as he stepped around Matthew. "We could have been away from here an hour ago, but you chose to make my friend here break into your safe. You could have been more accommodating, but you couldn't bring yourself to do the right thing, could you? You caused us a considerable amount of trouble."

He stopped behind Matthew, who was simply staring straight ahead as if he was waiting for something to happen.

"I'm a man of my word," Cole continued. "If I say that I'll spare someone, then I spare them. Equally, if I say that there'll be punishment, then I'm afraid punishment must follow. I'm sure you understand that kind of approach, it can't be very different to how things work in the business world. And if you know anything about this town at all, you know that I have a reputation to maintain. When people hear my name, they rightly feel fear in their chests, because they know that I get what I want. They know that when I say something has to happen... Well, it happens."

Reaching into his pocket, he took out one of the larger shards of glass that had earlier been picked up from the floor.

"No!" Stella shouted, but Gary continued to hold her back.

"Three million euros," Cole purred. "Is that worth a life?"

Matthew continued to stare straight ahead for a moment, before slowly turning to Stella. After all the laughter and mania, he was suddenly very calm.

"He won't do it," she told him, although her voice was filled with fear. "I promise..."

Above, in one of the upstairs rooms of the house, something bumped heavily.

"I told you it couldn't be changed," Matthew said, keeping his eyes fixed on Stella. "There was never even the slightest chance. Believe me, I tried from time to time, but there was no hope. That was the hardest thing to live with, really. The hope. You'll find out what I mean soon enough."

Again, something bumped loudly in one of the upstairs rooms, a little harder this time.

"Forgive her," Matthew added, with a hint of tears in his eyes, "she's got it harder than most. You see, she's the one who's had to witness this all happen in the right order. That's why she's going to be so angry."

Stella opened her mouth to reply, but in that instant Cole slashed the glass across Matthew's throat. Hearing a loud tearing sound as the flesh ripped open, Stella could only watch in horror as blood began to gush from the wound. Somehow Matthew was still managing to stare at her, even as his body shook violently and as blood continued to spray across the floor.

"No!" Stella sobbed, trying to reach toward him even though she knew she was too late. "Stop! Please..."

Cole let go of Matthew and stepped back. Somehow, managing to stay upright, Matthew continued to watch Stella, and after a few seconds his lips began to move.

"I'm sorry," Stella said, with tears streaming down her face. "This is all my fault! I'm so sorry..."

Matthew's lips moved slightly, but no words left his mouth. He almost toppled over, but he managed to stay up for a moment longer before finally slumping down to the side and landing dead in a pool of his own blood.

"You didn't have to do that!" Stella screamed, finally breaking free from Gary and rushing across the room.

Dropping to her knees, she rolled Matthew over, but she could already tell that she was too late. His dead, glassy eyes stared up toward the ceiling as another creaking sound rang out elsewhere in the house, and now the flow of blood had almost completely stopped.

Stella still checked for a pulse, just in case by some miracle he might have survived, but far too much blood had already spilled out.

"That's just the way things have got to be," Cole said firmly, towering above them both with the glass still in his right hand. "He had a choice. He'd still be alive, if only he'd listened to me."

"You didn't have to hurt him!" Stella said, slowly getting to her feet and turning to him. She could feel the rage starting to boil in her body.

"I saw no alternative," Cole told her. "Sometimes, when it comes to these things, one has to be cutthroat." He paused, before grinning. "Literally!"

"You're a murderer!" Stella yelled, rushing at him and slamming her fists against his chest, trying to beat him back. "You're nothing but a cold-blooded killer!"

"Gary," Cole said calmly, "will you get this woman away from me before I actually start to dislike her?"

Gary hurried over and tried to pull Stella back. He struggled for a moment, but he finally dragged her away. She tried to twist free, before dropping to the floor as tears streamed down her face. Looking over at Matthew's corpse, she saw the bloodied gash on his throat and realized that he was dead because she'd brought a bunch of criminals straight to his door. She thought of all the times she could have done things differently, all the choices she could have made that would have left Matthew Thorne alive, and she struggled to understand how she'd managed to rack up so many mistakes.

"This is all my fault," she whispered, as a cold shudder passed through her body. "All of it. I made this happen."

"We should go," Gary suggested, "before -"

Suddenly a loud creaking sound rang out, followed by a firm thud that seemed to be coming from somewhere upstairs.

"What the hell was that?" Cole asked, taking a couple of steps toward the doorway as he watched the ceiling.

A moment later, they all heard the clear sound of somebody walking across one of the upstairs rooms. A few seconds after that a door slammed shut, with such power that any other presence in the house was clearly no longer trying to hide itself away.

"Is someone else here?" Walter said, before turning to Stella. "Didn't this guy live alone?"

"His wife died years ago," Stella replied, as she felt a growing sense of fear in her chest.

"Babe, is there something you forgot to mention?" Gary hissed, pulling her closer. "You said this dude was a total loner. You were shitting me about that, were you?"

"It's her," Stella whispered.

"Hey!" Walter yelled, storming through into the hallway and then stopping to look toward the stairs. "Whoever else is in this house, you'd damn well better show your face right now or there *will* be consequences!"

"I don't like surprises," Cole sneered.

"Did you hear me?" Walter shouted, raising his voice even higher. "You'd damn well better -"

Before he could finish, a loud ripping sound rang out. Stella looked around trying to figure out what was happening, but a moment later she saw Walter step back just as the chandelier in the hallway came crashing down. Hundreds of glass decorations smashed against the hallway's marble floor, and chunks of metal fell to the side as the final trailing wires dropped down close to the bottom of the stairs.

"What the fuck?" Walter stammered, having been missed by just a few inches. "Did you see that?"

He turned and stepped back into the doorway.

"Did you see what just happened?" he asked, with a growing sense of incredulity as a smile began to spread across his face. "I could have been -"

In a flash, one of the metal pieces from the broken chandelier flicked up and flew up behind him, instantly decapitating him and sending his head cracking down onto the floor. As Walter's body toppled over with blood spraying from the top, his head rolled across the room before coming to a halt with his dead eyes staring straight ahead. His eyes blinked once, his mouth moved and let out a faint grown, and then he fell still.

A fraction of a second later, all the lights in the house switched off, plunging the entire building into darkness.

"It's her," Stella said again, as she heard another bumping sound coming from out in the hallway, perhaps from the top of the stairs. "You killed her husband. I don't think she's going to like that."

CHAPTER TWENTY-FIVE

"WHAT THE ACTUAL FUCK is all this bullshit?" Cole asked, his voice thick with tension as he looked down at Walter's severed head. "What is this place?"

Crouching down, he stared into Walter's lifeless eyes, as if he couldn't quite believe what had happened. After a moment he carefully reached out and picked the head up, and he held it for a few seconds before letting it drop back down with a sickening thud.

"You said this place isn't defended," he sneered at Gary. "What the hell kind of shit is *this*?"

"It's his wife," Stella said, listening for another hint of the ghostly presence.

"What wife?" Gary snapped, grabbing her

and forcing her to turn to him. "Babe, you're seriously starting to freak me out right now. Can we please rewind to the part where you start making sense again?"

"Martha Thorne died several years ago," she told him. "She's been haunting the place, but I don't think she made herself known very much. That might have just changed."

"Are you seriously talking about a dead woman?"

"I think she -"

Suddenly Gary slapped her hard around the face. She almost fell, but she somehow managed to stand firm.

"I know you're not trying to tell me that there's a ghost here," Gary said breathlessly, clearly starting to panic. "Stella, let's maintain a grip on reality and try to focus on what's actually going on. What kind of security contingent did this asshole actually have? Are we talking trained security? Is it just one dude, or are there several, or -"

"It's a dead wife," Stella said firmly, interrupting him. "I don't think any of us are going to get out of here very easily."

"Fuck this!" Cole shouted, before pulling a gun from his pocket and storming into the hallway. Aiming high, he fired a couple of shots toward the top of the stairs, blasting chunks away from the railing. "Do you think you can pull this shit on me? Whoever you are, you'd better have balls of steel, 'cause you're gonna need them if you're coming for Cole Archer!"

"He's got no idea what he's facing," Stella said, watching as Cole strutted about waving his gun in the air. "He thinks he can shoot his way out of this."

"Stop!" Cole yelled, before firing several more shots toward the top of the stairs. He kept pulling the trigger until the gun was empty, and he immediately began to reload. "I saw you up there!" he called out. "Do you think this is some kind of game? Do you seriously think you've got any chance at all, if you don't come down with your hands up right now?"

He waited, and then he stormed back through to join Stella and Gary.

"Here," he said, shoving the gun into Gary's hands, "go and flush this fucker out."

"But -"

"Do you know how to follow orders?" Cole continued, leaning closer to him. "In case you didn't notice, my best friend just got his head sliced off, and I'm telling you to get up there and find the bastard responsible. Or are you too much of a chicken?"

Aiming the gun at Gary's face, he waited for an answer.

"Sure," Gary stammered. "I mean, I guess I could -"

"Alive or dead, I don't care," Cole said, shoving the gun into his hands, "but I want that motherfucker to pay. If you don't kill him, at least drag him down here so I can do the job slowly and painfully. Or her. Whatever, it doesn't matter. Do you understand me?"

"Yes," Gary said, "but -"

"So move!"

Shoving him hard, Cole glared at Gary.

"Don't do this," Stella said, as she began to realize that Gary was going to obey. "We have to get out of here right now and go as far away from this house as possible. I don't know what she's capable of, but she's already killed one person and I don't think she'll stop until she's taken revenge on everyone she thinks is responsible for Matthew's death. If there's no -"

Before she could finish, Cole grabbed her by the scruff of the neck, and shoved her against the wall.

"No-one needs to hear this horseshit!" he sneered, before looking over his shoulder. "Gary, either you go up there and find whoever killed Walter, or I'll do the job. I should warn you, though, that if I have to do it, then I really won't see any need to keep you or your dumb little girlfriend around. Do you understand what I'm getting at here?"

"Yes," Gary stammered, taking a step back with the gun in his right hand. "Of course, I'll go and..."

His voice trailed off.

"Now!" Cole roared.

After muttering something under his breath, Gary turned and hurried out into the hallway.

"No!" Stella screamed, desperately struggling to get away from Cole's grip. "Gary, stop! You don't know what you're -"

Suddenly Cole slammed her face against the wall, shutting her up, and then he spun her around.

"Gary!" she shouted, with blood gushing from her cut lip.

"Shut up!" Cole sneered, before punching her and sending her slamming back against the wall. "You really don't know when to stay quiet, do you?"

Gasping as she slumped to the floor, Stella immediately tried to cover her face to protect against another strike. As she did so, however, Cole grabbed her by the throat and turned her around, before crushing his knee against her chest.

"I don't want to hear your bullshit about ghosts," he said firmly, as he took hold of her left arm and began to twist, almost ripping it from the socket. "I've killed a lot of people," he added, as the pain became stronger and Stella began to whimper, "and believe me, when someone's dead, they stay -"

Before he could get another word out, Cole's head exploded, splattering blood and bone and brain matter all across the wall.

Frozen for a moment, struggling to understand what was happening, Stella stared at what was left of Cole's head, until finally his body toppled back and hit the floor. Only now, as blood dribbled down the wall next to her, was Stella able to see Gary standing in the middle of the room with the gun raised. Even from a distance, she could see that his hand was starting to shake.

"He just popped," he stammered, clearly in shock. "Like a watermelon. He just blew right open."

Turning, Stella saw a couple of broken teeth sliding down the wall, caught up in the pinkish-red gunk that had burst out from inside Cole's skull. Less than sixty seconds earlier, all that matter had been clumped together, producing thoughts and words and actions, and now it was all sprayed across a patch of particularly ugly wallpaper, revealed for the first time to the moonlight that was streaming through a nearby window.

"He had it coming," Gary said, hurrying over and helping Stella up. "I was willing to put up with a lot of his shit, but I wasn't going to stand by and let him hurt you."

She turned to him.

"I never should have listened to him," he continued. "I let him dazzle me with all that talk of money and power, when all I really need in the world is you. I know you probably think I can't change, you might even be right, it might be impossible for people to truly change, but I swear I'm going to try. I won't blame you if you still don't want anything to do with me, but at least let me help you get out of here for good."

He paused, waiting for an answer, before reaching down and grabbing the original bag of fifty thousand euros that Matthew had given Stella earlier in the evening.

"Take this," he added, pressing it into her hands, "and start a new life. Go north, and never come back to Nice again."

With that, he grabbed her hand and began to lead her out of the room. As they reached the hallway, however, they both heard a shuffling sound coming from somewhere nearby, and they stopped to look around.

"I think I saw her just now," Gary said, with fear in his voice. "Just after Cole sent me out here, and before he started hurting you, I saw a woman standing at the top of those stairs." He used the gun to point toward the landing high above. "I really only saw her silhouette, but it was definitely there and then suddenly it was gone."

Hearing a creaking sound, they both backed against the wall and looked around the dark hallway.

"Is it true?" Gary continued. "Is there a ghost here?"

"It's the ghost of Matthew Thorne's dead wife Martha," Stella explained, watching for any sign that the dead woman might be about to appear, "and I really don't think we should stick around to find out too much. Let's just get out of here."

She paused, before squeezing Gary's hand tight.

"Together."

Stepping away from the wall, they made their way around the huge, smashed chandelier and headed toward the front door. One of the other bags of cash, with hundreds of thousands of euros spilling out, had been left on the floor in the middle of all the broken glass and twisted metal, but they ignored all of that as they opened the front door and stepped out to the steps at the front of the house. A cool breeze blew against them both, and Stella stopped as soon as she saw the lights of Nice glittering in the distance.

"I wasn't sure she'd let us leave," she said, turning to Gary, "or -"

Suddenly an agonized, ear-piercing scream rang out from somewhere in the house.

"That was a woman," Gary pointed out, his voice filled with fear. "It didn't sound real, it was like -"

"Come on," Stella said, still holding his hand as she led him down the steps. "We can be out of town by the time the sun comes up."

"Wait!"

She stopped again, but Gary had stopped first and his hand slipped out of hers.

"There was a bag right by the door," he told her, taking a couple of steps back up toward the house. "I only have to reach inside."

"Gary, no!" she hissed, still holding the smaller bag. "Let's just go!"

He hesitated, before hurrying to the door and reaching down, grabbing the larger bag and quickly shoveling as much of the money inside as possible. He glanced across the hallway, watching to make sure that there was no sign of Martha Thorne in the darkness, and then – after shoving the last of the money into the bag, he stepped back and turned to look down toward Stella.

"There must be half a million in here," he said with a relieved sigh, holding the bag up for her to see. "Babe, we've really earned this. We're gonna -"

Stopping suddenly, he seemed frozen in place.

Stella waited for him to continue, and then she held out a hand.

"Hurry!" she called out. "Gary, the money doesn't matter, let's just go and -"

In that instant, she saw that something was on his face. In the moonlight, she was just about able to make out small shapes reaching around from behind, and after a few seconds she realized what she was seeing.

Fingers.

Pale, rotten fingers.

"Babe?" Gary said, his voice tense with fear now as his head tilted back slightly. "I can feel... it's so cold... they're freezing, they..."

Stella opened her mouth to reply, but she was starting to make out a face glaring at her from directly behind Gary, and she could only watch as the ghostly figure spread its fingers further across his face.

"Is it her?" Gary gasped, as Martha Thorne tightened her grip on his head. "Babe, is it the ghost?"

"I..."

"Is it her?" he asked again. "Stella, I can't move. Babe, please, just tell me..."

As Martha's hands tightened again, Stella heard the woman's cold, dead fingers creaking in the moonlight.

"Please don't hurt him," she whispered, with tears running down her face. "Please, I know you must hate us all, but I'm begging you to let him go."

"Is it her?" Gary sobbed. "Babe, just tell me. Is it -"

Twisting suddenly, Martha snapped his neck, breaking the bones with a loud, jagged crunch.

"No!" Stella screamed, rushing forward, but she tripped on the bottom step and dropped down hard, landing on her knees. Looking up toward the top of the steps, she was horrified to see Gary's glassy eyes staring at her as Martha Thorne held him up.

"Run," he gasped with the last breath of his

life. "Babe..."

A moment later, Martha's fingers clicked as they released Gary's head, and finally his body slumped to the ground and toppled down the steps, landing right next to Stella.

"Gary," Stella whispered, touching the side of his face. She knew he was dead, and she could feel her heart breaking. "I'm here, I..."

Before she could finish, she heard a faint gasping sound. Looking up, she was horrified to see Martha towering above her. For a few seconds, unable to move at all, Stella could only stare into the dead woman's eyes. A moment later, Martha began to slowly walk down toward her. Finally, hearing Gary's voice echoing in her mind, telling her once more to run, Stella scrambled to her feet and raced away across the dark driveway.

CHAPTER TWENTY-SIX

Six months later...

"MUM, CAN I HAVE a burger for lunch?"

"You had a burger yesterday," Amanda said with a sigh, as she lay on the sun lounger with a large hat covering her face, "and the day before. Aren't you sick of them by now?"

"No," Ashley said, furrowing his brow. "I'm on holiday and it's our last full day and I almost never have what I want to eat when we're at home. Can I please have a burger?"

"Fine," Amanda replied, "take some money from my purse. But tonight you're having a proper meal at dinner, do you understand? With vegetables and everything, and no arguments!"

"Yeah, okay," he said eagerly, opening the

purse and pulling out a twenty euro note.

"Oh, and Ashley?" Amanda called out as her son raced toward the bar.

He stopped and looked back at her.

"Order one for me as well," she said, still not even opening her eyes as she basked in the midday sun. "Sweet potato fries, and extra ketchup. Don't forget cutlery."

***

As other children screamed in the pool, splashing one another as they played, Ashley made his way toward the bar area. His bare feet splashed against puddles of water, and – as usual – he carefully avoided stepping on any of the plastic drains that dotted the area. As he reached the bar he saw that a man was in the middle of ordering, so he stopped and waited.

After a few seconds, he noticed that the drunk woman was there again.

Although he tried not to look, Ashley couldn't help turning his head slightly. The woman, who always wore a blue two-piece bikini and always sat slumped on a stool at the end of the bar, had her head in her hands as usual as a half-finished beer sat next to her ashtray. Ashley had begun to really look out for the woman, since she'd been there when he and his mother had arrived at the hotel and he'd heard a few people mention that she was basically living at the place. Apparently she paid cash every week.

The idea of living at a hotel made Ashley feel so jealous. He couldn't imagine anything better.

Suddenly the woman jerked up and looked around, as if she'd woken from a daze. Her tired, bloodshot eyes blinked a couple of times, and after a few seconds she turned directly to Ashley.

Feeling guilty for having been watching the woman, Ashley turned and looked at the man at the counter, who was still running through his order. Ashley was starving now, but the man seemed to be taking forever, clearly placing an order for an entire family.

"Hey, Miguel," the drunk woman called out, before downing the last of her beer. "Another one of these whenever you're ready."

The barman nodded at her, but he kept his focus on the man.

"It's okay, I can wait," the woman muttered, clearly irritated, before squinting slightly as she looked at Ashley again. "Another burger?"

For a moment, Ashley considered pretending that he hadn't noticed her, but then he nodded shyly.

"Good choice, kid," she continued, as she picked a small fly from her plastic beer cup. "That and the mac cheese are the only things I ever eat from this place."

Ashley offered a faint smile, just to be polite, and then he looked up at the man at the counter again. He couldn't quite understand how it took some people so long to place a simple order for some food and drink.

"You're heading home tomorrow, right?" the woman asked.

Ashley turned to her again.

"It's alright," she continued, "I was talking to your mum last night in the main bar." She nodded toward the hotel. "I think she'd already put you to bed, but we had a few drinks and talked about life. You're flying back to Luton, right?"

"We live in Greenwich," Ashley said awkwardly.

"Yeah, she told me," the woman replied. "I miss London. Man, I used to think it was so dull, but now I wouldn't mind going back. Even if it was just for a visit, I'd love to walk along Oxford Street and see Hyde Park again, do a few touristy things, take in some shows, see some friends." She paused, with a faraway look in her eyes as if she was remembering some long-ago better time in her life. "Drink in an English pub," she added softly. "It's the little things you miss. The escalators. The smell of an underground train. The sound of traffic outside a pub by Trafalgar Square."

Ashley waited for her to continue, but the

woman seemed lost in her memories. He didn't mind that at all, although – as he turned to look at the bar – he was annoyed to see that the man was *still* discussing some aspects of his order.

"Hey, kid," the woman said suddenly, "can I ask you a question?"

Ashley looked at her again.

"Have you ever stolen anything?"

Surprised, Ashley wasn't entirely sure what to say.

"There's no right or wrong answer," the woman continued, slurring her words slightly. Even at midday, she was already clearly drunk. "Come on, you're a kid, you must have stolen something at least once in your life. Everyone does."

Ashley thought for a moment, before shaking his head.

"Really?" the woman asked, sounding disappointed. "Are you having me on right now? Can't you think of even one thing that you've stolen in your entire life?"

"No," Ashley said cautiously.

"Are you some kind of little saint?" she continued, raising a skeptical eyebrow. "Is that it? Turn around, I wanna see if you've got, like, angel wings on your back."

Before he had to think of an answer, Ashley saw that the man at the counter had finally walked away. Filled with relief, he hurried to take the man's spot, and he held the twenty euros up for the barman.

"Two burgers, please," he said, aware that the drunk woman was keeping an eye on him. "One with sweet potato fries. And two orange juices."

"Are you gonna give your mum all the change?" the woman asked.

"Stella," the barman said, turning to her, "leave the kid alone, okay? I'll get to you in a minute. Honestly, it might do you good to wait a little while before your next drink."

"You love me being here," the woman said with a smile, as she watched the barman tap Ashley's order into the console. "If I wasn't here, who'd you have to talk to all day? Everyone else is way too busy having fun. Admit it, having me here has made this the best summer you've ever spent doing this job, hasn't it?"

The barman rolled his eyes as he looked down at Ashley and took the money.

"Do you ever feel like you're going round and round in circles?" the drunk woman asked, still watching Ashley. "Round and round, never stopping, all these loops and stuff that we think are straight lines."

"I won't warn you again," the barman said, turning and glaring at her. "I don't mind you being here -"

"Thanks a lot!"

"But don't annoy my customers," he added firmly. "Especially not the young ones. If you keep bugging this kid, I'll have security toss you out, and then where will you go?"

"You're no fun today, Miguel," she replied, feigning great sadness. "I'm used to you being a little bit mean, but you're going way too far. Who hurt you? Is there anything I can do to make you feel better?"

"There's your change," the barman said, ignoring her as he set some coins in Ashley's hand, "and your drinks, and I'll bring the food over to you and your mum just as soon as it's ready."

"Thank you," Ashley said, carefully not looking at the drunk woman as he turned to go back over to the sun loungers.

"Skim the change," the woman whispered as Ashley passed her. "Your mum'll never know. Hell, she's probably expecting it. Don't be a little angel all your life. Experience the thrill of nicking a few cents here and there. Be like me!"

Ignoring her, Ashley picked his way around the drains and walked past the packed swimming pool. The drunk woman had seemed particularly irritable during his latest encounter, and he didn't like what she'd said about stealing the change. Stopping as he reached his mother's sun lounger, he was careful to put every last coin back into her purse, and then he turned and shielded his eyes from the sun as he looked back toward the bar.

The drunk woman was already slumped back down, apparently nodding off even as the barman placed another full pint of beer on the counter next to her elbow.

CHAPTER TWENTY-SEVEN

"WELL DONE," AMANDA SAID, after taking another sip of wine, "you ate all your vegetables."

Ashley smiled, although deep down he felt as if he was being patronized. His mother always acted as if it was a big deal when he ate his vegetables at dinner, despite the fact that he actually *liked* carrots and green beans. He didn't even mind broccoli.

"So I'm going to pop into the bar after dinner," Amanda continued, "just for a wind-down drink to mark the end of the trip. You'll be okay reading in the room, won't you?"

"Sure," Ashley replied, even though he hated being left alone in the room every night. He knew his mother liked to sit in the bar and talk to men. "I'll be fine."

"Back to London tomorrow," she said with a sigh, before sliding the key over to him. "We've got to make the most of the holiday, right?"

***

Stepping out of the elevator, Ashley turned to head straight to the room. His feet padded softly against the hotel's carpet, but after just a few steps he came to a halt as he realized he could hear a sobbing sound coming from somewhere up ahead. He watched the corridor, but he could already tell that the sound seemed to be coming from round the next corner.

"Keep away from me!" a woman's voice snapped suddenly, followed by a scrabbling sound. "I know you're there! Don't come near me!"

Although he wasn't certain that the woman was talking to him, Ashley preferred to not take any chances. He knew he could get to the room if he went the other way; the walk would be much longer, but at least he wouldn't have to go around that particular corner and see what was happening. He always tried to avoid confrontation, so finally he turned to follow the circuitous route to the room.

"Hey!" the voice hissed. "You!"

Stopping again, Ashley looked over his shoulder, and he was surprised to see the drunk woman peering at him. She was on her hands and knees, leaning around the next corner and watching him with an intense stare.

"Did you see her?" the woman asked.

"Who?" Ashley replied.

She looked both ways, as if she expected to spot somebody else at any moment.

Ashley hesitated, before turning to walk away.

"Did you see her?" the woman called out again, and then she got to her feet and ran up behind him. Grabbing him by the shoulders, she forced him to turn and look up at her. "You must have done. She was right here!"

"I don't know who you're -"

"I know she's here," the woman replied, once again looking both ways along the corridor. "She's been getting closer. I knew this was going to happen. I knew she'd find me eventually."

Looking up at the woman's eyes, Ashley couldn't help but feel that she seemed to be completely insane. Not only was she constantly turning to look in every direction, but her lips were moving slightly as if she was whispering something silently to herself, and a few seconds later she spun around and bumped back against the wall as if she'd heard movement nearby.

"Show yourself!" she yelled. "Why are you doing this to me? Just get it over with!"

"I have to go," Ashley said, turning to walk

away.

"No!" the woman snapped, grabbing him by the arm. "I need you to tell me if you see her too!"

"I don't want to," he replied, trying to twist away.

"I don't care what you want!" she told him.

"You're hurting me!"

"I don't give a crap!" she yelled, suddenly slamming him against the wall and then pinning him in place, pushing her arm against his throat. "Martha Thorne is coming for me!" she sobbed, as tears ran down her face. "She's been coming for me all along! I don't know why it's taken her all this time, I don't know if she walked here or something stupid like that, but she's never going to give up! I didn't even take most of the money, I only took the bag Matthew had already agreed to give me!"

"I want to -"

"And I didn't hurt him!" she continued. "Why can't she see that? I know she might think that it's my fault, but the people who actually hurt him are already dead! I'm sorry, I never meant for it to end like that, but she can't seriously think that I have to pay! And I can't sleep, not unless I'm drunk! How is anyone supposed to live like this?"

Looking both ways, Ashley was already trying to figure out how to escape.

"I'll show you!" the woman said, grabbing his wrist and dragging him along the corridor.

"I want to go to my room!" he shouted.

"Right there!"

Forcing him to stop, she grabbed his chin and turned his head so that he could see along the next corridor.

"I swear I saw her," she stammered. "It was only for a second, but she was staring right at me. Do you think she's toying with me? Is that it?" She turned Ashley's head so that he was looking at her again. "Is she that cruel? Is she just teasing me so that eventually I'll break down in fear? I lost Gary, I miss him so much. Isn't that enough punishment?"

"I want to go to my room," Ashley said, and now he too had tears in his eyes.

"I didn't hurt him!" she shouted along the corridor. "Do you hear me? I'm sorry about what happened to Matthew, but you can't blame me! I didn't want to go back to the house that night!"

She waited, and then she looked over her shoulder.

"This isn't fair," she whimpered. "I never meant to end up like this. I wanted to be a good person. I just wanted to live an honest life, I never set out to do anything bad, it all just snowballed and before I knew it, I was here. I only wanted to -"

Suddenly Ashley twisted free and ran. He felt the woman try to grab his arm, but he slipped away and raced along the corridor, clattering into the wall at the first turn but somehow managing to keep going. At the turn after that, he dared to look over his shoulder, and he saw the crazy woman running after him. He turned and hurried to the door to the hotel room, and then he fumbled with the key for a moment before finally managing to get inside. As he turned and slammed the door shut, the woman reached out, but she was too late.

"Hey!" she hissed, tapping on the other side of the door as Ashley took a couple of steps back. "Kid, seriously, I need your help. I can't trust my own eyes anymore, I don't know what's real and what's just in my head. Can I borrow you for just a few minutes? I just need to know whether she's really here, or whether I'm going out of my mind."

She fell silent for a moment.

Ashley waited, not daring to move.

"Please?" she added, and now her voice was cracking as she began to sniff back more tears. "I'm so scared. If I run, I'll only have to face her somewhere else. I can't live like that. Can you help me?"

She began to scratch at the door, but a few seconds later she let out a horrified gasp.

"She's coming!" she whimpered. "I can see her! She's walking right toward me! Kid, come out and tell me whether this is real, or whether it's all in my head!"

Still standing in the dark hotel room, Ashley looked at the bottom of the door and saw a dark patch where the woman was kneeling on the floor outside. After a moment, however, the patch disappeared and he heard the woman running away.

"Don't come near me!" he heard her shouting in the distance. "I didn't do anything wrong!"

With that, she was gone, leaving Ashley standing in silence. He was terrified that the woman might return, but then he realized he could hear another set of footsteps out in the corridor. Somebody else was walking slowly and calmly along the corridor, but they stopped as soon as they were outside the door. Looking at the floor again, Ashley could see a dark patch. He felt sure that the drunk woman couldn't have gone all the way round and returned, but after a few seconds he stepped toward the door and stood on the tips of his toes so that he could see through the peephole.

A pale, dark-eyed woman was standing on the other side of the door, staring straight back at him. For a moment Ashley was frozen in place, and then the woman turned and walked away.

Pulling back, Ashley stumbled and fell against the side of the bed. He told himself that there was no need to be scared, but he couldn't stop thinking about the two strange women he'd seen since leaving his mother downstairs. Taking a deep breath, he tried to focus on the fact that he was safe now, and that he wasn't going to risk opening the door again until his mother returned.

CHAPTER TWENTY-EIGHT

SITTING ALONE IN THE gloomy hotel room, with the wet bikini still clinging to her body, Stella stared at the half-open door and waited for the sound to return.

In the distance, happy families were playing in the pool, splashing and laughing and yelling, but Stella had managed to ignore most of that noise and instead she was laser-focused on the door. She knew that the sound had been real, and that it had been moving steadily closer, and she also knew that there was no point running. After all, she'd tried running before, and how had that turned out?

A moment later she heard a scratching sound coming from the hallway, and she instantly tensed. She was on the verge of shivering, but not because of the cold fabric of her bikini. Instead, sheer terror had frozen her bones, and she knew only too well the face of the creature out in the hallway. The scraping sound was moving closer, and she knew that she'd finally run out of places to hide.

Suddenly she heard a faint gasp, and she instantly pulled back on the bed.

Somewhere outside, a child screamed, followed by a heavy splashing sound. The scream was nothing bad, just the squeal of a kid who was playing. More screams followed, while Stella sat in deathly silence and listened to the sound of the *thing* making its way along the corridor. She knew that at any moment, the old familiar face would appear and she'd see a pair of dead eyes staring back at her. She also knew, deep down, that she was too tired and scared to try running again.

"Please," she whispered, still watching the door, "just -"

Before she could finish, the scratching sound came to an abrupt halt. She felt a growing sense of nausea in the pit of her stomach, and she couldn't help but picture the awful sight that was waiting on the other side of the door. The effects of all the poolside alcohol had worn off; she was perfectly sober, and her heart was racing, and for the first time in many months she was once again having to remember to breathe.

Slowly, with a deep creaking sound, the

door began to swing open.

Reaching down, Stella clutched the side of the bed as she waited for the inevitable sight. Had she ever really believed that she might escape? Perhaps at the start, at least when she'd managed to numb her fears with alcohol. Now, however, she knew that this moment had been coming for so very long. She'd never really had a chance of escaping.

The door swung open all the way. Outside, another child screamed.

"What are *you* doing here?" Stella asked.

Holding the bag he'd been sent back up to fetch, Ashley stared at her.

"Forget it," Stella continued, once again having to remember to breathe. Each time, she felt the effort required to take a breath in, then to take a breath out, then to take another in. "I know she's out there. It's time. There's nothing I can do now to get away from her. I should have known that right from the start."

Ashley looked both ways along the corridor.

"I can't explain," Stella said. "Just go. I'm sorry about last night, I shouldn't have grabbed you like that. I shouldn't have pulled you into all of this. You're heading home today, right?"

Ashley paused, before nodding.

"We've got the morning in the pool," he explained, "and then we're getting taken to the airport."

"Say hi to the old place for me, will you?" Stella said, with tears glistening in her eyes. "I'd love to go, but... I know it doesn't matter how far I run. She's going to find me. She's coming right now. Isn't it better to just... get it over with?"

Ashley looked along the corridor again.

"There's no-one here," he said cautiously.

"She's really close," Stella replied with a terrified smile. "Like I said, I can't explain. Do you ever get the feeling that you've wandered into the end of someone else's story?"

Ashley thought about that for a moment, before turning and walking away.

"Because I do," Stella whimpered, as rotten fingers began to reach around from behind her head.

***

"Okay, the coach'll be here any minute now," Amanda muttered a few hours later, craning her neck to look along the road. "Don't worry, we've got plenty of time before check-in even opens."

Turning, Ashley couldn't help but look once more at the police cars that had been parked for a while outside the front of the hotel. An ambulance had just pulled up as well, and anxious-looking porters kept hurrying in and out of the building. Something had been going on for about an hour, but all the guests had been told that there was no need to worry, and that they should just avoid going into a certain section of the hotel for a little while

Ashley watched as the hotel's manager hurried out of the main reception area and rushed over to where two police officers were talking.

"What's happening?" he asked, before looking up at his mother.

"I don't know," she said, as she took a puff on her cigarette. "Don't worry, it's none of our business. As long as that coach turns up soon, we'll be fine."

She stubbed the cigarette out.

"I'm just going to pop to the loo one more time," she added, hurrying past her son and up the stairs to the pool area. "If the coach comes, tell the driver I'll be back in one second."

Once his mother was gone, Ashley looked back over at the police cars. Several officers were milling about now, and the hotel manager seemed angry about something. A moment later, the main door opened and Ashley watched as two paramedics carried something out on a trolley. He could instantly tell that they had a body, and he could see that a sheet had been placed completely over the person, which he figured meant that they must be dead.

Taking a few steps forward, Ashley watched as the back of the ambulance was opened. The paramedics began to load the trolley inside, although they were struggling with something near one of the wheels and one of them was snapping angrily in French. Every time they tried to slide the trolley into the ambulance, something seemed to stick near the bottom of the mechanism, and now both the paramedics seemed to be getting increasingly annoyed.

Nearby, voices were shouting excitedly in the pool.

Suddenly the trolley tipped. The nearest paramedic reached out to stop it, but she was too late. The sheet fell away, just as the drunk woman's body fell off and landed hard on the tarmac.

Ashley let out a shocked gasp as he saw that the woman was too stiff to land naturally. She seemed frozen in the moment of her death, with her hands held up against her chest and her fingers curled tight; her eyes, meanwhile, were open and filled with terror, and her mouth was locked in a wide, silent scream. As the paramedics hurried to cover the woman again with the sheet, Ashley couldn't help but notice that there was a darkness around her eyes. Whatever had happened to her, she'd clearly been scared when she'd died.

"It's okay," the manager said suddenly, stepping in front of Ashley and guiding him away. "She just had a heart attack. It's nothing but a simple tragedy. Look, is that the coach you're taking to the airport?"

Ashley tried to peer back past him, to see the woman again, but she'd finally been loaded into the ambulance and a moment later the doors slammed shut.

"Great, it's here," Amanda said, hurrying down the steps. "I was starting to worry that I might need to call a taxi."

"Mum," Ashley said, turning to her, "a woman's dead."

"It's nothing," the manager said with a forced smile. "A minor matter that we're taking care of. A lady unfortunately passed this morning, I think she must have had a weak heart. Please, I hope that you've both had a wonderful time here at the hotel. I hope you'll consider coming back to us one day."

"Sure," Amanda replied, as the coach pulled up. "Thanks for everything. Come on, Ashley, let's get the bags in. I need to check a few emails on the way to the airport."

Although he desperately wanted to ask more questions about what had happened to the drunk woman, Ashley stayed quiet as his mother led him onto the coach. Once he was in his seat, he peered out the window and saw that the hotel's manager was talking to the police again. Looking over at the ambulance, which was starting to pull away, he couldn't help but wonder about the dead woman, and about why she'd seemed so scared. A moment later, as the coach set off and he watched the hotel disappearing into the distance, Ashley found himself thinking back to the woman's rambling claims about someone who was after her, and one line in particular stuck in his mind.

"Do you ever get the feeling," she'd asked him earlier that day, the last time he'd seen her, "that you've wandered into the end of someone else's story?"

CHAPTER TWENTY-NINE

Twenty years earlier...

"MATTY! WAIT UP!"

Stopping at the edge of the fairground, Matthew Thorne turned and saw that Luke was running after him. Laughs and screams rang out from the various rides nearby, and Matthew had to admit that he was glad to be away from the crush of people. Every year, he and his friends rushed to the fairground when it came to town, and every year Matthew felt more and more as if he was too old for the place; now, having just turned eighteen, he could think of many other things he'd rather be doing on a hot summer's afternoon. Working on his business plans, for example, and planning for his future.

"Hey, Matty," Luke said a little breathlessly as he finally caught up. "You're not going already, are you? There's still so much we haven't done."

"I told you," Matthew replied, "I'll meet you later."

"Don't you want to visit the fortune teller?"

"Why would I ever do that?" he asked.

"Because it's fun," Luke said matter-of-factly. "Come on, don't be a total downer. I want to see her, but I'm not going by myself."

"Then you're a wimp."

"Please?" Luke continued, with a trace of a whine in his voice. "I'll pay, and I'll buy you a drink after as well." He waited for an answer. "I know you like to sit around planning how you're going to become a millionaire," he added, "but can't we at least have a little bit of fun first?"

Matthew opened his mouth to say that he was busy, but at the last moment he spotted the fortune teller's tent nearby. He really wanted to go and work on one of his projects, yet after a few seconds he realized that he didn't want people to start talking again about him being boring. He knew he'd gained something of a reputation in that regard, and he wanted to push back a little.

"Fine," he said. "Why not? What harm can it do?"

***

"This is so corny," Matthew whispered a short while later, once he and Luke were in the tent and had been shown to their seats. "It's like every cliché ever, all packed together in one place."

"She might hear you!" Luke hissed, watching the empty seat opposite, waiting for the fortune teller to arrive. "Do you really want to get on her bad side?"

"What's she going to do?" Matthew asked, rolling his eyes. "Is she going to curse me or something?"

Before Luke could reply, they both heard a rustling sound and turned just in time to see a woman stepping through to join them. Wearing a red shawl, and with several gold rings around her wrists, the woman strongly resembled the painted figure on the advertising board outside, and Matthew couldn't help but smirk as he glanced over at Luke once more.

"Seriously?" he whispered.

"Before we start," the woman said calmly, "I must inform you that I'm picking up some very strong energy from one of you. Very *strange* energy. I mention this not because I wish to scare you, but because I have a policy of scrupulous honesty."

"What kind of strange energy?" Luke asked.

"I think we'll be fine," Matthew said, still struggling to contain his mirth. "Can we just get on with it?"

"You're in a hurry?" the woman replied, turning to him.

"I just want to get it done," he explained.

"You're the one whose energy troubles me," she said as she took a seat. "Yes, I'm picking it up more clearly by the second. I can read the fortune of your friend, but for you, it will be impossible. You are one of those rare souls with a less linear direction."

"A less linear direction?" Matthew said, raising a skeptical eyebrow. "Is that a bad thing?"

"Some souls become knotted," she replied. "My special area of expertise is in the matter of reincarnations. When I read somebody's fortune, I see not only the rest of this life, but also the journey their souls will take after death."

"So you can tell me if I'm going to come back as a squirrel?" Matthew asked jokingly.

"Hey, we should take this seriously," Luke cautioned him.

"I'm taking it *very* seriously," Matthew countered, while keeping his gaze fixed on the woman. "Apparently I have a twisted soul. Does that have any side-effects?"

"It means that some of your incarnations can overlap," she explained. "Often, they will be drawn to one another. They will *find* one another. The condition is rare, but when it happens, the result is usually a cluster of three simultaneous incarnations in a relatively small area."

"Let me try to get this straight," Matthew said cautiously. "Are you claiming that you can tell how someone's going to be reincarnated?"

"I don't claim this. I know it."

"Fine, and you're saying that in my case, my soul might have already been reincarnated in another person who's walking around right now, and I might... meet them?"

"And that is why I can't read your fortune," she told him. "To do so would be to invite disaster. When I encounter such souls, I always leave them alone. If you were to become aware of your other incarnations, the results would be catastrophic."

"Well now you've actually got my attention," he said with a faint smile, before holding his hands out across the table. "Come on, do me first."

"I already -"

"I insist," he continued. "We all know how this works. Or are you after more money?"

"There's not enough money in the world to make me read your fortune," she told him, before turning to Luke. "You, on the other hand, are -"

"I'm telling you to read my goddamn fortune," Matthew said firmly. "I already paid, you have an obligation to deliver the service you advertised."

"You'll be refunded your money."

"I want you to read my fortune!"

"And I'm saying that I will not," she replied. "When incarnations touch, the risk is far too severe. You're better off not knowing. Now, if you'd like to wait while I look into your friend's future, that would be -"

"This is bullshit," Matthew said, getting to his feet. "We can both see through you. You're nothing but a charlatan, and no amount of nonsense is going to change that. I've got to admit, you're a little more inventive than I expected, but all this talk of doom and gloom isn't going to wash. You're nothing but a fraud."

He paused, before turning and heading toward the door.

"Come on, Luke," he added, "let's get our money back and leave this dumb bitch to get on with her scam."

"Wait!" the woman snapped.

Matthew stopped and turned to her.

"I'll read your fortune," she said through gritted teeth. "So long as you acknowledge that I warned you of the consequences, I suppose I have no further obligations regarding your safety. It's only yourself you'll be putting at risk."

"Then how can I resist?" he asked with a faint chuckle, before returning to the table and sitting back down, then holding his hands out.

"Come on, you old witch." He wiggled his fingers, as if to invite her to touch. "I've got to admit, you might not be so bad at this scam as I thought. You've managed to wind me up enough to make me interested."

The woman glanced briefly at Luke, before reaching out and taking hold of Matthew's hands.

"I'm going to give you one last chance to back out," she told him. "After this point, there will be no going back, no chance to unlearn what you are about to discover. I have heard of men driven mad by this process, of people who can't handle the knowledge of what they are to become. There are many who believe that it's better to live in ignorance rather than -"

"You don't need to keep selling me on this," Matthew said, interrupting her. "I've just got one question. Can people be reincarnated as anything?"

"Any living thing, yes," she told him. "Your soul can inhabit any body, male or female, human or otherwise."

"Could I be a tree?" he asked.

"Are you going to keep on with all these stupid questions?" Luke said with a sigh. "This was just supposed to be a bit of fun, Matty, not some kind of exercise in philosophy. Trust you to take something simple and ruin it. I should have just come here by myself."

"I want to know what I'm going to come

back as," Matthew said firmly, still watching the woman. "I want to hear whatever bullshit she comes up with next."

"I think it's time to get on with the reading," she replied. "Assuming you're still determined to go ahead, that is."

"Oh, I'm ready," he said with a grin, before squeezing her hands tight. "I wouldn't miss this for the world!"

CHAPTER THIRTY

"MATTY? ARE YOU OKAY?"

Suddenly opening his eyes, Matthew let out a loud gasp and began to lean forward, only to realize at the last second that he was flat on his back. Startled and disorientated, he looked around, and after a few seconds he finally came to understand that he was on the floor of the tent, with Luke and the fortune teller staring down at him.

"Dude, what happened?" Luke continued. "You totally spaced out there for a moment! I thought you were having a fit!"

Matthew blinked a couple of times, aware of a strange fuzziness in his mind. He felt terrified, yet he had no idea what might have caused that fear; he could tell that he'd forgotten something important, something that just a few seconds earlier had filled his thoughts. As he began to sit up, and as Luke helped him lean against the side of the table, he struggled to put his memories back together.

"You were rambling like a total madman," Luke told him. "Seriously, I couldn't make sense of anything you were coming out with. You kept going on about some big house, and someone called Martha, and also someone called Gary, and all this other stuff and -"

"Shut up!" Matthew hissed, as he felt those names starting to revive something in his thoughts.

"So were you just messing around?" Luke asked. "If you were, it was very -"

"I told you to shut up!" Matthew shouted, before getting to his feet. His hands were trembling, and he couldn't help but worry that he might be about to collapse at any moment. After a few seconds, he turned to the fortune teller. "What did you do to me?" he sneered.

"I warned you that -"

"Did you drug me?" he asked. "Is that it?"

"You didn't drink or eat anything here," she pointed out.

"Then it was some kind of gas!"

"Dude, what are you going on about?" Luke asked. "Okay, you're actually starting to freak me out a bit. You were talking for a few minutes, and then you just went on about all that random stuff, and then you tipped off the chair and hit the deck."

Matthew turned to him.

"No-one drugged you," he added. "Matthew, seriously, you just flew off on one, all by yourself."

Matthew opened his mouth to reply, but for a few seconds he was unable to find any words. Staring at the fortune teller, he still felt as if all sorts of thoughts had begun to fill his mind, but he had no idea how to put them together. He'd always prided himself on being calm and collected; for the first time in his life, he worried he was on the verge of tumbling into chaos.

"When a knot like this occurs," the fortune teller said softly, "it usually results in three simultaneous incarnations. They might not begin and end at the same time, but there will come a point at which they come close together. From what I was able to make out just now, it would seem that you, Matthew, are the second of these three incarnations, which means that there was one that you have already experienced and one that you will experience once this life is over."

"I felt pain," he stammered. "Immense pain, running through me, but I don't know where it was coming from."

"That is likely your next incarnation, but the details will be vague. You will have learned a great deal more about the incarnation that came *before* this one."

"I remember... a beach," he said, as some of

his thoughts began to coalesce. "I remember the heat. I remember living in great fear, and trying to escape from something."

"I shouldn't have gone through with this," the fortune teller said with a sigh. "I allowed myself to be guided by my emotions, when I should have been more resolute."

"I remember a hotel," Matthew continued, as he tried yet again to cling to the fragments of memory that were drifting through his thoughts, "and I remember a piano playing. I remember dinner, and I remember a dark road with a the lights of a city in the distance. And I remember another hotel, and a pool, and I was sitting at the bar and..."

"It's always objects and places that are clearest," the fortune teller told him. "At first, anyway."

"I was in a beautiful house," he added, "but it didn't belong to me. I was a guest, I was visiting someone, but I can't quite remember his..."

As his voice trailed off, Matthew tried desperately to remember more. After a few seconds, however, he shook his head and began to make his way toward the exit.

"It was a dream, that's all," he said angrily. "I listened to you too much, you got into my head with all your stupid stories and you actually tricked me into believing it for a moment."

"Let me help you," Luke said, hurrying over

to try to support him, only to get immediately pushed aside.

"I don't need help!" Matthew snapped, although he immediately had to reach out and support himself against the side of the door. "I *never* need help. Just give me a moment and I'll be able to get out of here under my own steam."

"You might not think that any of this really happened," the fortune teller said, watching him carefully, "but that'll change. You won't be able to deny the truth forever. And when you come to terms with whatever you saw, you should understand that you can't change anything. What happens is simply what happens. The fact that you've seen it means that it has already taken place. That's why many people find the experience of seeing their other lives so... haunting."

"I'm not haunted by anything."

"You will be."

"Save the dramatic crap for someone who actually gives a damn."

With that, Matthew stumbled out of the tent.

"He's really not into that kind of spiritual stuff," Luke said after a moment. "I only brought him here as moral support."

"I regret letting your friend goad me into giving him a reading," the fortune teller replied, before slowing turning to him. "Eventually he'll have to come to terms with this new knowledge.

And when he does, he'll be very lucky if he survives with even a shred of his sanity intact."

***

"There you are!" Luke said a few minutes later, as he spotted Matthew kneeling on the ground near the edge of the fairground. "Man, you really gave me a fright in that tent!"

"I remember," Matthew said, sweating profusely as he stared at the ground. "It's becoming clearer, I was living a completely different life. I was in Nice, in France, and -"

"That doesn't sound too bad," Luke said jokingly.

"And my name was Stella," he added.

"Stella?" Luke furrowed his brow for a moment. "Dude," he said cautiously, "are you saying... were you... a *woman* in a previous life?"

"The fortune teller said we can be anything," he pointed out. "Anything alive. I was a woman named Stella in my previous life, and I was living in Nice with my boyfriend, and we were hustlers. We scammed people to try to keep our heads above water, I hated the lifestyle but I put up with it because I was in love. Then things got pretty dicey with some local gangsters and..."

Luke waited for him to continue.

"She was right," Matthew whispered.

"About the knot... I *did* meet myself. I had no idea what was happening, but I met myself and I saw..."

Again, his voice trailed off.

"You saw what?" Luke asked, still hoping against hope that his friend was simply playing some kind of prank. "Come on, you're not into this sort of stuff. You don't actually believe a word that woman told you, do you?"

"I saw..."

Matthew continued to stare at the ground for a moment longer, before slowly turning to him with a horrified expression on his face.

"I saw my own death," he said finally.

"Are you out of your mind?"

"I saw my throat being cut," he said, reaching up and touching his throat as he thought back to the sight of the knife ripping through his flesh. "I saw my blood spraying from the wound. I saw my own dead body on the floor. I had no idea at the time, but now I understand. I knew. I mean, *he* knew. I mean, I saw the man that I am now, and I saw in his eyes that he knew what was about to happen."

He turned to Luke.

"Then I ran. I ended up in La Rochelle, hiding from something, but it caught up with me and..."

For a moment, he remembered the sensation of the dead woman's hands on his face, reaching around from behind.

"She found me," he added, as his voice began to tremble. "Poor Martha, I'd never told her about any of this. All she saw was a bunch of criminals murdering me. She must have been so angry. I died, and I must have been reborn in this body, except somehow I was twisted back to an earlier time. So now I'm living this life, and I've already seen how it's going to end."

Still convinced this his friend had to be joking, Luke watched him carefully.

"Dude," he said after a few seconds, "I don't mean to be funny, but everything you just told me... I mean, it's completely insane. Do you even realize how many impossible things you're asking me to believe? You can't be serious. Come on, you're freaking me out. That fortune teller was nuts. Let's go and get breakfast and a pint, and we can laugh about all of this."

"I won't let it happen," Matthew said, before getting to his feet and clenching his right fist. "I know what she claimed, about it being inevitable, but I refuse to believe that." He squeezed his fist even tighter. "I'm not going to let that be my future. I'm in control of my own destiny. I'm not going to become that man!"

CHAPTER THIRTY-ONE

Several years later...

STEPPING INTO THE BAR, Matthew Thorne looked around and saw that none of his friends had arrived yet. On just the first day of a two week skiing holiday in Switzerland, he was exhausted and full of aches already, but he told himself that a whiskey would help him feel a little better.

"On the rocks, please," he said to the waiter, before glancing around again.

This time, he made eye contact with a woman sitting nearby, and he was immediately struck by her beauty. He knew he should look away, but he felt utterly shocked, until finally the woman managed a faint smile.

"Sorry," Matthew said, worried that he

might be blushing. "I didn't mean to stare."

"No, it's fine," she replied. "I was staring too, right?"

She paused for a moment.

"My friends are late," she explained.

"Mine too."

"So I look like a total loser, sitting here all by myself."

"Snap."

An awkward silence settled between them for a moment. Finally, Matthew – who usually found himself pretty tongue-tied around women – took his drink and made his way over to the woman.

"Would you like some company?" he asked, mesmerized by her beautiful green eyes.

"I wouldn't say no to that," she replied with a grin.

"There's just one thing," he continued cautiously, "before I sit down. I know this might sound odd, but... do you mind telling me your name?"

"That doesn't seem particularly odd," she said, before reaching a hand out toward him. "Rosie Ashton, at your service."

"Rosie," he replied, with an obvious sigh of relief, as he shook her hand. "That's a really beautiful name."

***

Five hours later, having mostly ignored their friends, Matthew and Rosie were still talking as the waiters began to close the bar. Midnight had already rolled around, but Matthew had barely noticed the time pass at all, since he and Rosie had spent the entire time chatting away. Now, as they wandered out of the bar and stopped on the terrace to look out at the mountains, there almost seemed to be something magical in the air.

Although he knew he had to play things cool, Matthew understood deep down that he was in love.

"So I think I might have heard of you after all," Rosie said cautiously. "I remember reading about a guy named Matthew Thorne who made millions and who's famous for being something of a workaholic. Tell me, how did your buddies drag you out here for a holiday?"

"I just like trying different things," he told her. "To be honest, I try to never stay on the same path for too long."

"You like to be in control of your own destiny, huh?"

"Something like that."

"Do you *believe* in destiny?" she continued.

"That's a complex question," he pointed out. "To be honest, I believe that we're all capable of making choices every day that can change our futures massively. I don't think anything's set in stone." He looked up at the vast array of stars in the night sky high above. "I think we have as many choices as there are stars. More, even. When I look out at the infinite beauty of the cosmos, I just find it impossible to believe that we're trapped down here with no way to make our own destiny."

"I'd like to agree with you."

"Then do," he said with a smile. "In fact, I think -"

Before he could finish, Rosie surprised him by stepping closer and kissing him gently on the lips. The kiss was brief, but she stayed close and a moment later they kissed more passionately.

"I'm sorry," she said as she finally pulled back, "I just couldn't help myself. I never normally do anything like that."

"Me neither," he admitted.

"Tonight just feels different somehow."

"I know what you mean," he replied. "So, Rosie, where exactly do you live?"

"I'm based in London," she told him, "but work takes me around a lot. I work for a corporate events management company, so pretty much every month I have to head off to somewhere in Europe. I was in Amsterdam last week, and a few weeks before that I did Oslo and Copenhagen in one day."

"That sounds... busy."

"I really like traveling," she continued. "I

like seeing the world from different perspectives. Even if I'm really only passing through, it's fun to get little snapshots of other cultures."

She paused, before checking her watch.

"Hey," she added, "so I have a really early start in the morning and -"

"Will you go to dinner with me?" he asked, blurting the question out before he'd really had time to consider what he was saying. "Back in London, I mean. When we're both there. One evening."

She paused, biting her bottom lip for a moment, before smiling and nodding.

"I'll be back next week," he told her.

"As will I," she replied, before reaching into her pocket and pulling out a business card. "This has my number and email on it, so just get in touch and we'll figure something out. Just so you know, I eat absolutely anything, I'm not remotely picky, so why don't you take me to your absolutely favorite place? I don't care if it's posh or expensive, I just want to go somewhere you really love. And then, if we go on a second date, I'll return the favor."

"Sounds good to me," he admitted, before looking down at the card.

"One more thing," she added, grabbing his hand to stop him. "This is going to sound really dumb, but I told a little white lie earlier. I've had trouble with guys in the past, they always try to add me on social media, so I have this stupid and probably very annoying habit of..."

Her voice trailed off, and then she kissed him on the cheek before taking a step back.

"My name's not really Rosie," she admitted. "You'll see my real name on the card. If that's not a deal-breaker, and if you don't think I'm completely out of my mind, I look forward to hearing from you."

As she walked away, Matthew already knew that he was deeply and truly in love. At the same time, he could also feel a slow sense of dread starting to crawl through his chest. He knew he had to look at the business card, but he held off for a few more seconds before turning it over and reading the name. In that moment, he felt the chains of the universe wrapping tight around his heart.

Martha Stone

"Martha," he whispered, having avoided any contact with that name for so very long.

He paused, and then he began to laugh. Although he felt utterly horrified, he knew that he loved this girl far too much to ever let her go, and he leaned back against the wall as he realized that all his efforts had been for nothing. He'd worked so hard to control his own destiny, to avoid the pitfalls that he remembered from his previous life, but he'd been led straight back to where he was supposed to be. And as he continued to look at the card, he slowly slid down until he was sitting on the floor, and he finally understood that all his attempts at freedom had been for nothing.

He could feel his mind starting to fall apart, and he found himself having to concentrate on trying to save some fragment of his sanity. He wanted to scream, but he knew that screaming wouldn't help, that by screaming his futility and rage he'd only end up inviting the universe to take more shots at his pathetic hopes and dreams. He told himself that he'd tried, that he'd genuinely done all he could, and that reality had simply refused to bend to his will.

He was going to marry Martha, and she was going to die, and then later he'd meet Stella in Nice. There'd also be a third incarnation of his soul at the time, although he had yet to figure that part out.

So he started laughing loud, and then even louder, even though he knew he should be crying. He was laughing at the absurdity of everything, and at the realization that even if he tried again and again to run away from his destiny, somehow it would always find a way to head him off. He was laughing, too, at the understanding that he *had* made his own choices, even if he'd somehow made them a long time earlier, and now he was unable to change what had happened. Although he couldn't quite get his mind around that idea, he still found himself laughing harder and harder at the sheer desperation of his situation. He knew he was going to call Martha when he got back to London, and that there was really no longer any point fighting the inevitable.

As he continued to laugh, all the stars of the night sky shone through the darkness.

CHAPTER THIRTY-TWO

Several years later...

"I'VE BEEN WAITING A long time for tonight," Matthew said softly, before furrowing his brow for a moment. "Do you believe in fate?"

Somewhat taken aback by that question, Stella wasn't quite sure how to answer. Fortunately the waiter had arrived with the starters, so she was able to take a few seconds to consider her response. Still, those seconds drained away quickly enough, leaving her still without any kind of witty response.

"I really don't know," she said finally, once the waiter was gone and steam from the soup began to rise past her face. "I haven't thought about it that much. I suppose I feel like everyone has a chance to shape their own destiny."

"But what if they don't?" he asked, his voice tense with what seemed to be fear. "Or what if they do, but once they've made their choices, there's no going back? What if time doesn't work the way we think it does?"

"I'm not -"

"Put it another way," he continued, leaning forward slightly, conspicuously ignoring his bowl of soup. "What if we have all the freedom we could ever want, but we can't change things that have already happened?"

"I suppose that's just life," Stella suggested awkwardly, still struggling to understand exactly what was wrong. She'd dismissed the idea that Matthew might be on drugs, but something about him seemed so very different. "You make a choice, and then you have to deal with the consequences. Believe me, there are some things I'd like to change if I could."

"Yes, but what if..."

He paused, and then he sighed.

"This soup smells really nice," Stella said, hoping to shift the topic of conversation onto a lighter topic. "I've never really been into soup, but this is great. What was it again? Parsnip and -"

"What if you already knew the choices that you'd made?" Matthew asked, interrupting her. "What if you have to live through them again, except this time you couldn't change what you'd done before?"

"I've never really been into philosophy a whole lot," she told him, and she was starting to feel stupid. She'd never paid a lot of attention at school, and she always felt inadequate whenever people talked about anything serious. "I just take things as they come, you know? I get on with my life and try not to overthink it too much."

"The day after my wife died, a butterfly landed on my desk," Matthew told her.

"Butterflies are cool."

"It was beautiful," he continued, "and I just sat and watched it for the longest time. It didn't fly away, it didn't seem to mind me at all. It just stayed there, right in the middle of the desk. Its wings were mostly blue, with a little black, and as I watched that butterfly I couldn't shake the feeling that it was watching me in return."

"It probably was," Stella agreed, with a nervous style. "I hope you don't mind, but I was hoping to talk to you about -"

"And I got to thinking," Matthew said, ignoring her, "about why that butterfly was there. What did it want? Why would it simply rest there on my desk, in my office, when it had a whole garden outside to explore? It had flown through the window and landed very deliberately, or at least that's the impression I got. The butterfly's presence was no accident. In that moment, I knew that the butterfly had arrived specifically to see me."

"Right," Stella said cautiously. "That sounds... cool."

"And this was the day after my wife had died," Matthew added. "That seems important somehow."

"You must have been feeling awful."

"I started to wonder whether the butterfly was a sign," he explained. "I know this might sound far-fetched, but it was as if the butterfly was in some way returning to me, and I began to think that my wife..."

Stella waited for him to finish.

"You think your wife was reincarnated as a butterfly?" she suggested finally.

"It crawled across the desk and onto my hand," he told her, "and in that moment, I felt so very free and happy. I can't explain the sensation, except to say that the butterfly found some way to make me feel as though life was worth living. And Martha had told me, before she died, that she'd come back if she could and give me some kind of sign. At the time, I just assumed that she was rambling, but her words returned to me as the butterfly sat on my hand. And then it flew away, straight back out the window, as if it's work was done."

"That's really nice," Stella said, figuring that she at least had to let him finish the story.

"But then I started thinking about the life cycle of the butterfly," Matthew continued. "It made no sense. Martha had died just the day before, and obviously the butterfly – at least in its caterpillar form – must have existed for longer than that. So it couldn't have been Martha, could it? Because their lives couldn't... overlap like that, could they? There's just no logic in that, unless..."

Again, Stella waited for him to finish, but this time he seemed to be lost in thought. She was starting to think that her opportunity had arrived.

"I need to ask you something," she said finally. "Something important."

"I'm sure you do," he replied, fixing her with a firm stare. "I've been waiting for you to tell me why we're here tonight."

"The thing is..."

Suddenly feeling tongue-tied, Stella tried to work out how exactly to explain her predicament. She didn't want to simply ask for the cash, yet in effect she knew there was only so much she could do to dress up her words as anything more noble.

"It's complicated," she managed to say finally, "but the real problem is that I'm in trouble." She paused, watching his face as she tried to judge his reaction. "A lot of trouble, actually," she continued, "and time's running out and I don't have anywhere else to turn. You don't know me, you have no reason to help me or to care about what happens to me, but I -"

"You need money."

She instinctively wanted to deny that suggestion, but she knew she had to be honest.

"I wouldn't ask," she explained, barely able to meet his gaze, "if this wasn't a situation that's really about life or death. Believe me, I know how wrong this all is, and I know how I sound, but the truth is that I'm desperate and -"

"And you need a lot of money or your boyfriend will be killed," Matthew said suddenly, interrupting her. "He's involved with some gangsters and their patience has run out, and they're going to make an example of him if he doesn't hand over the money he owes by midnight tonight. They've already roughed him up, they could have killed him by now, but in desperation you're here to try to get the money by any means possible. You know he can't simply run away, you know you need every euro he owes, and you saw it sitting in my safe. That's pretty much the situation, right?"

Staring at him open-mouthed, Stella had no idea how he'd managed to figure out so much.

"Well, I -"

"So now we have to go to the house to *fetch* the money," Matthew said through gritted teeth. He seemed increasingly agitated, and after a moment Stella noticed that he was gripping the sides of the table. A moment after that, he got to his feet, nudging the table in the process. "That's the plan, isn't it?" he continued. "There's no way out, so we might as well just get it over and done with right now."

"I just -"

"There's no point delaying, is there?" he asked, his voice trembling slightly. Was it fear, or anger, or both? "There are no other possibilities. We both know what has to happen, so we should just get on with it."

"You don't *have* to help," she pointed out.

"Don't I?"

"Well, no," she replied, trying to figure out why he was reacting so strangely. "You can tell me to leave. You can swear at me and kick me out and call me all sorts of names."

"Would that change anything?"

"What do you want in return?"

"For the money?" He paused, fixing her with a glare that made her feel extremely uncomfortable. "I don't know that there's anything I can possibly ask for," he continued. "That ship has sailed, and now there's really nothing to do except let things unravel as they must."

"Right," Stella said cautiously, still not quite understanding the strange sense of doom that seemed to have filled every fiber of his being. "So does that mean..."

She paused, struggling to believe that her

plan had really worked.

"Does that mean," she continued finally, "that you're going to help us?"

"What choice do I have?" he asked. "There's no point delaying this for even a moment longer, Stella Ward. It's time for us to go back to the house." He paused for a moment, eyeing her with a curious gaze. "Are you ready?"

"The house?"

She swallowed hard.

"I... guess so," she said cautiously, even though she'd hoped to find some way to avoid ever setting foot in the place again. Still, she knew she couldn't exactly argue.

"This way," he replied, as he led her away from the table. "Do you know the strange thing? I was once told that these things come in threes, but that's the only part I've never been able to work out. There's you, and there's me, so where's the third of us?"

"I'm not sure what you mean."

"Forget it," he said. "I'm rambling. So, tell me... do you ever get the feeling that you've arrived late, at the end of somebody else's story?"

EPILOGUE

A few days earlier...

BUZZING FRANTICALLY, SLOWLY TURNING in circles around the pin that had pierced its abdomen, the wasp tried desperately to get free.

"Look at the stupid little bastard," Gary said, squinting as he lifted his sunglasses and leaned closer to take a better look. "He's just going round and round."

Still the wasp tried to escape. The pin ran straight into its yellow-and-black striped body and held it stuck to a piece of rotten wood on the side of the pier leg. The buzzing sound was non-stop now and the wasp continually tried to fly away, as if it failed to understand how it was being held down.

"It's going to rip its belly open at this rate,"

Gary continued with a grin. "The poor bastard doesn't even realize that."

"Abdomen," Stella said.

"What?"

He turned to her.

"It's called the abdomen," she replied, lounging on the sand with a book propped against her knees, before turning to him. "That part of the insect, I mean. Their bodies have three parts.. There's the head, the thorax and the abdomen. We learned about it in school."

"Whatever."

"Can't you put it out of its misery?" she asked. "Why did you even do that to the poor thing, anyway?"

"Because I could," Gary told her. "Because it's a dumb bug and it doesn't know any better. It needs to learn who's above it on the food chain. Anyway, it was annoying me. It kept flying around and getting in my way. Stupid little bug."

He looked past her for a moment and watched tourists splashing in the sea, and he felt a shiver of disgust run through his bones. Nice was filled with tourists at the height of summer, and they crowded onto the beaches in such numbers that he sometimes wondered how they could all fit. His attention was briefly caught by a man wandering past, hawking cups of fruit along with various inflatables. Gary scrunched his nose for a couple of seconds, secure in the knowledge that no matter how bad things might get, he'd never be as lowly as some poor sod who made a living selling crap to holidaymakers.

"When did you suddenly give a damn, anyway?" he added, glancing at Stella again. "About bugs, I mean."

"Fine," she said with a sigh, turning to the next page of the book before giving up and setting it aside. "I swear, I'm roasting out here. I feel like all the water's just evaporating from my body. Can't we go somewhere else?"

"You don't like being on the beach now?"

"I think I'm going to dehydrate to death." She sat up on the sand. "Seriously, I'm tanned enough already."

"A little extra never hurt anyone," he suggested. "It's cheaper than using fake stuff, and you know all those rich guys love it." He reached over and put a hand on her knee. "Gotta keep thinking about the money. If you look at it a certain way, you're at work right now, getting that cute little body of yours into perfect condition."

"Can we go?" she asked. "Please? Just for an hour or two."

"Go where?"

"I don't know," she said with another sigh, as heat from the midday sun continued to beat down and force sweat from her brow. "Anywhere."

Down on the rotten chunk of wood, the wasp was still pinned in place, twitching – and trying to escape from the burning sun – in its final moment of agony.

THE HAUNTING OF MATTHEW THORNE

Also by Amy Cross

The Haunting of Nelson Street
(The Ghosts of Crowford book 1)

Crowford, a sleepy coastal town in the south of England, might seem like an oasis of calm and tranquility. Beneath the surface, however, dark secrets are waiting to claim fresh victims, and ghostly figures plot revenge.

Having finally decided to leave the hustle of London, Daisy and Richard Johnson buy two houses on Nelson Street, a picturesque street in the center of Crowford. One house is perfect and ready to move into, while the other is a fire-ravaged wreck that needs a lot of work. They figure they have plenty of time to work on the damaged house while Daisy recovers from a traumatic event.

Soon, they discover that the two houses share a common link to the past. Something awful once happened on Nelson Street, something that shook the town to its core.

Also by Amy Cross

The Revenge of the Mercy Belle
(The Ghosts of Crowford book 2)

The year is 1950, and a great tragedy has struck the town of Crowford. Three local men have been killed in a storm, after their fishing boat the Mercy Belle sank. A mysterious fourth man, however, was rescue. Nobody knows who he is, or what he was doing on the Mercy Belle... and the man has lost his memory.

Five years later, messages from the dead warn of impending doom for Crowford. The ghosts of the Mercy Belle's crew demand revenge, and the whole town is being punished. The fourth man still has no memory of his previous existence, but he's married now and living under the named Edward Smith. As Crowford's suffering continues, the locals begin to turn against him.

What really happened on the night the Mercy Belle sank? Did the fourth man cause the tragedy? And will Crowford survive if this man is not sent to meet his fate?

Also by Amy Cross

The Devil, the Witch and the Whore
(The Deal book 1)

"Leave the forest alone. Whatever's out there, just let it be. Don't make it angry."

When a horrific discovery is made at the edge of town, Sheriff James Kopperud realizes the answers he seeks might be waiting beyond in the vast forest. But everybody in the town of Deal knows that there's something out there in the forest, something that should never be disturbed. A deal was made long ago, a deal that was supposed to keep the town safe. And if he insists on investigating the murder of a local girl, James is going to have to break that deal and head out into the wilderness.

Meanwhile, James has no idea that his estranged daughter Ramsey has returned to town. Ramsey is running from something, and she thinks she can find safety in the vast tunnel system that runs beneath the forest. Before long, however, Ramsey finds herself coming face to face with creatures that hide in the shadows. One of these creatures is known as the devil, and another is known as the witch. They're both waiting for the whore to arrive, but for very different reasons. And soon Ramsey is offered a terrible deal, one that could save or destroy the entire town, and maybe even the world.

Also by Amy Cross

The Soul Auction

"I saw a woman on the beach. I watched her face a demon."

Thirty years after her mother's death, Alice Ashcroft is drawn back to the coastal English town of Curridge. Somebody in Curridge has been reviewing Alice's novels online, and in those reviews there have been tantalizing hints at a hidden truth. A truth that seems to be linked to her dead mother.

"Thirty years ago, there was a soul auction."

Once she reaches Curridge, Alice finds strange things happening all around her. Something attacks her car. A figure watches her on the beach at night. And when she tries to find the person who has been reviewing her books, she makes a horrific discovery.

What really happened to Alice's mother thirty years ago? Who was she talking to, just moments before dropping dead on the beach? What caused a huge rockfall that nearly tore a nearby cliff-face in half? And what sinister presence is lurking in the grounds of the local church?

Also by Amy Cross

Darper Danver: The Complete First Series

Five years ago, three friends went to a remote cabin in the woods and tried to contact the spirit of a long-dead soldier. They thought they could control whatever happened next. They were wrong...

Newly released from prison, Cassie Briggs returns to Fort Powell, determined to get her life back on track. Soon, however, she begins to suspect that an ancient evil still lurks in the nearby cabin. Was the mysterious Darper Danver really destroyed all those years ago, or does her spirit still linger, waiting for a chance to return?

As Cassie and her ex-boyfriend Fisher are finally forced to face the truth about what happened in the cabin, they realize that Darper isn't ready to let go of their lives just yet. Meanwhile, a vengeful woman plots revenge for her brother's murder, and a New York ghost writer arrives in town to uncover the truth. Before long, strange carvings begin to appear around town and blood starts to flow once again.

Also by Amy Cross

The Ghost of Molly Holt

"Molly Holt is dead. There's nothing to fear in this house."

When three teenagers set out to explore an abandoned house in the middle of a forest, they think they've found the location where the infamous Molly Holt video was filmed.

They've found much more than that...

Tim doesn't believe in ghosts, but he has a crush on a girl who does. That's why he ends up taking her out to the house, and it's also why he lets her take his only flashlight. But as they explore the house together, Tim and Becky start to realize that something else might be lurking in the shadows.

Something that, ten years ago, suffered unimaginable pain.

Something that won't rest until a terrible wrong has been put right.

AMY CROSS

Also by Amy Cross

American Coven

He kidnapped three women and held them in his basement. He thought they couldn't fight back. He was wrong...

Snatched from the street near her home, Holly Carter is taken to a rural house and thrown down into a stone basement. She meets two other women who have also been kidnapped, and soon Holly learns about the horrific rituals that take place in the house. Eventually, she's called upstairs to take her place in the ice bath.

As her nightmare continues, however, Holly learns about a mysterious power that exists in the basement, and which the three women might be able to harness. When they finally manage to get through the metal door, however, the women have no idea that their fight for freedom is going to stretch out for more than a decade, or that it will culminate in a final, devastating demonstration of their new-found powers.

AMY CROSS

Also by Amy Cross

The Ash House

Why would anyone ever return to a haunted house?

For Diane Mercer the answer is simple. She's dying of cancer, and she wants to know once and for all whether ghosts are real.

Heading home with her young son, Diane is determined to find out whether the stories are real. After all, everyone else claimed to see and hear strange things in the house over the years. Everyone except Diane had some kind of experience in the house, or in the little ash house in the yard.

As Diane explores the house where she grew up, however, her son is exploring the yard and the forest. And while his mother might be struggling to come to terms with her own impending death, Daniel Mercer is puzzled by fleeting appearances of a strange little girl who seems drawn to the ash house, and by strange, rasping coughs that he keeps hearing at night.

The Ash House is a horror novel about a woman who desperately wants to know what will happen to her when she dies, and about a boy who uncovers the shocking truth about a young girl's murder.

Also by Amy Cross

Haunted

Twenty years ago, the ghost of a dead little girl drove Sheriff Michael Blaine to his death.

Now, that same ghost is coming for his daughter.

Returning to the small town where she grew up, Alex Roberts is determined to live a normal, quiet life. For the residents of Railham, however, she's an unwelcome reminder of the town's darkest hour.

Twenty years ago, nine-year-old Mo Garvey was found brutally murdered in a nearby forest. Everyone thinks that Alex's father was responsible, but if the killer was brought to justice, why is the ghost of Mo Garvey still after revenge?

And how far will the real killer go to protect his secret, when Alex starts getting closer to the truth?

Haunted is a horror novel about a woman who has to face her past, about a town that would rather forget, and about a little girl who refuses to let death stand in her way.

AMY CROSS

Also by Amy Cross

The Curse of Wetherley House

"If you walk through that door, Evil Mary will get you."

When she agrees to visit a supposedly haunted house with an old friend, Rosie assumes she'll encounter nothing more scary than a few creaks and bumps in the night. Even the legend of Evil Mary doesn't put her off. After all, she knows ghosts aren't real. But when Mary makes her first appearance, Rosie realizes she might already be trapped.

For more than a century, Wetherley House has been cursed. A horrific encounter on a remote road in the late 1800's has already caused a chain of misery and pain for all those who live at the house. Wetherley House was abandoned long ago, after a terrible discovery in the basement, something has remained undetected within its room. And even the local children know that Evil Mary waits in the house for anyone foolish enough to walk through the front door.

Before long, Rosie realizes that her entire life has been defined by the spirit of a woman who died in agony. Can she become the first person to escape Evil Mary, or will she fall victim to the same fate as the house's other occupants?

AMY CROSS

Also by Amy Cross

The Ghosts of Hexley Airport

Ten years ago, more than two hundred people died in a horrific plane crash at Hexley Airport.

Today, some say their ghosts still haunt the terminal building.

When she starts her new job at the airport, working a night shift as part of the security team, Casey assumes the stories about the place can't be true. Even when she has a strange encounter in a deserted part of the departure hall, she's certain that ghosts aren't real.

Soon, however, she's forced to face the truth. Not only is there something haunting the airport's buildings and tarmac, but a sinister force is working behind the scenes to replicate the circumstances of the original accident. And as a snowstorm moves in, Hexley Airport looks set to witness yet another disaster.

AMY CROSS

Also by Amy Cross

The Girl Who Never Came Back

Twenty years ago, Charlotte Abernathy vanished while playing near her family's house. Despite a frantic search, no trace of her was found until a year later, when the little girl turned up on the doorstep with no memory of where she'd been.

Today, Charlotte has put her mysterious ordeal behind her, even though she's never learned where she was during that missing year. However, when her eight-year-old niece vanishes in similar circumstances, a fully-grown Charlotte is forced to make a fresh attempt to uncover the truth.

Originally published in 2013, the fully revised and updated version of *The Girl Who Never Came Back* tells the harrowing story of a woman who thought she could forget her past, and of a little girl caught in the tangled web of a dark family secret.

AMY CROSS

Also by Amy Cross

Asylum
(The Asylum Trilogy book 1)

"No-one ever leaves Lakehurst. The staff, the patients, the ghosts... Once you're here, you're stuck forever."

After shooting her little brother dead, Annie Radford is sent to Lakehurst psychiatric hospital for assessment. Hearing voices in her head, Annie is forced to undergo experimental new treatments devised by a mysterious old man who lives in the hospital's attic. It soon becomes clear that the hospital's staff, led by the vicious Nurse Winter, are hiding something horrific at Lakehurst.

As Annie struggles to survive the hospital, she learns more about Nurse Winter's own story. Once a promising young medical student, Kirsten Winter also heard voices in her head. Voices that traveled a long way to reach her. Voices that have a plan of their own. Voices that will stop at nothing to get what they want.

What kind of signals are being transmitted from the basement of the hospital? Who is the old man in the attic? Why are living human brains kept in jars? And what is the dark secret that lurks at the heart of the hospital?

AMY CROSS

BOOKS BY AMY CROSS

1. Dark Season: The Complete First Series (2011)
2. Werewolves of Soho (Lupine Howl book 1) (2012)
3. Werewolves of the Other London (Lupine Howl book 2) (2012)
4. Ghosts: The Complete Series (2012)
5. Dark Season: The Complete Second Series (2012)
6. The Children of Black Annis (Lupine Howl book 3) (2012)
7. Destiny of the Last Wolf (Lupine Howl book 4) (2012)
8. Asylum (The Asylum Trilogy book 1) (2012)
9. Dark Season: The Complete Third Series (2013)
10. Devil's Briar (2013)
11. Broken Blue (The Broken Trilogy book 1) (2013)
12. The Night Girl (2013)
13. Days 1 to 4 (Mass Extinction Event book 1) (2013)
14. Days 5 to 8 (Mass Extinction Event book 2) (2013)
15. The Library (The Library Chronicles book 1) (2013)
16. American Coven (2013)
17. Werewolves of Sangreth (Lupine Howl book 5) (2013)
18. Broken White (The Broken Trilogy book 2) (2013)
19. Grave Girl (Grave Girl book 1) (2013)
20. Other People's Bodies (2013)
21. The Shades (2013)
22. The Vampire's Grave and Other Stories (2013)
23. Darper Danver: The Complete First Series (2013)
24. The Hollow Church (2013)
25. The Dead and the Dying (2013)
26. Days 9 to 16 (Mass Extinction Event book 3) (2013)
27. The Girl Who Never Came Back (2013)
28. Ward Z (The Ward Z Series book 1) (2013)
29. Journey to the Library (The Library Chronicles book 2) (2014)
30. The Vampires of Tor Cliff Asylum (2014)
31. The Family Man (2014)
32. The Devil's Blade (2014)
33. The Immortal Wolf (Lupine Howl book 6) (2014)
34. The Dying Streets (Detective Laura Foster book 1) (2014)
35. The Stars My Home (2014)
36. The Ghost in the Rain and Other Stories (2014)
37. Ghosts of the River Thames (The Robinson Chronicles book 1) (2014)
38. The Wolves of Cur'eath (2014)
39. Days 46 to 53 (Mass Extinction Event book 4) (2014)
40. The Man Who Saw the Face of the World (2014)

AMY CROSS

41. The Art of Dying (Detective Laura Foster book 2) (2014)
42. Raven Revivals (Grave Girl book 2) (2014)
43. Arrival on Thaxos (Dead Souls book 1) (2014)
44. Birthright (Dead Souls book 2) (2014)
45. A Man of Ghosts (Dead Souls book 3) (2014)
46. The Haunting of Hardstone Jail (2014)
47. A Very Respectable Woman (2015)
48. Better the Devil (2015)
49. The Haunting of Marshall Heights (2015)
50. Terror at Camp Everbee (The Ward Z Series book 2) (2015)
51. Guided by Evil (Dead Souls book 4) (2015)
52. Child of a Bloodied Hand (Dead Souls book 5) (2015)
53. Promises of the Dead (Dead Souls book 6) (2015)
54. Days 54 to 61 (Mass Extinction Event book 5) (2015)
55. Angels in the Machine (The Robinson Chronicles book 2) (2015)
56. The Curse of Ah-Qal's Tomb (2015)
57. Broken Red (The Broken Trilogy book 3) (2015)
58. The Farm (2015)
59. Fallen Heroes (Detective Laura Foster book 3) (2015)
60. The Haunting of Emily Stone (2015)
61. Cursed Across Time (Dead Souls book 7) (2015)
62. Destiny of the Dead (Dead Souls book 8) (2015)
63. The Death of Jennifer Kazakos (Dead Souls book 9) (2015)
64. Alice Isn't Well (Death Herself book 1) (2015)
65. Annie's Room (2015)
66. The House on Everley Street (Death Herself book 2) (2015)
67. Meds (The Asylum Trilogy book 2) (2015)
68. Take Me to Church (2015)
69. Ascension (Demon's Grail book 1) (2015)
70. The Priest Hole (Nykolas Freeman book 1) (2015)
71. Eli's Town (2015)
72. The Horror of Raven's Briar Orphanage (Dead Souls book 10) (2015)
73. The Witch of Thaxos (Dead Souls book 11) (2015)
74. The Rise of Ashalla (Dead Souls book 12) (2015)
75. Evolution (Demon's Grail book 2) (2015)
76. The Island (The Island book 1) (2015)
77. The Lighthouse (2015)
78. The Cabin (The Cabin Trilogy book 1) (2015)
79. At the Edge of the Forest (2015)
80. The Devil's Hand (2015)
81. The 13th Demon (Demon's Grail book 3) (2016)
82. After the Cabin (The Cabin Trilogy book 2) (2016)
83. The Border: The Complete Series (2016)
84. The Dead Ones (Death Herself book 3) (2016)

85. A House in London (2016)
86. Persona (The Island book 2) (2016)
87. Battlefield (Nykolas Freeman book 2) (2016)
88. Perfect Little Monsters and Other Stories (2016)
89. The Ghost of Shapley Hall (2016)
90. The Blood House (2016)
91. The Death of Addie Gray (2016)
92. The Girl With Crooked Fangs (2016)
93. Last Wrong Turn (2016)
94. The Body at Auercliff (2016)
95. The Printer From Hell (2016)
96. The Dog (2016)
97. The Nurse (2016)
98. The Haunting of Blackwych Grange (2016)
99. Twisted Little Things and Other Stories (2016)
100. The Horror of Devil's Root Lake (2016)
101. The Disappearance of Katie Wren (2016)
102. B&B (2016)
103. The Bride of Ashbyrn House (2016)
104. The Devil, the Witch and the Whore (The Deal Trilogy book 1) (2016)
105. The Ghosts of Lakeforth Hotel (2016)
106. The Ghost of Longthorn Manor and Other Stories (2016)
107. Laura (2017)
108. The Murder at Skellin Cottage (Jo Mason book 1) (2017)
109. The Curse of Wetherley House (2017)
110. The Ghosts of Hexley Airport (2017)
111. The Return of Rachel Stone (Jo Mason book 2) (2017)
112. Haunted (2017)
113. The Vampire of Downing Street and Other Stories (2017)
114. The Ash House (2017)
115. The Ghost of Molly Holt (2017)
116. The Camera Man (2017)
117. The Soul Auction (2017)
118. The Abyss (The Island book 3) (2017)
119. Broken Window (The House of Jack the Ripper book 1) (2017)
120. In Darkness Dwell (The House of Jack the Ripper book 2) (2017)
121. Cradle to Grave (The House of Jack the Ripper book 3) (2017)
122. The Lady Screams (The House of Jack the Ripper book 4) (2017)
123. A Beast Well Tamed (The House of Jack the Ripper book 5) (2017)
124. Doctor Charles Grazier (The House of Jack the Ripper book 6) (2017)
125. The Raven Watcher (The House of Jack the Ripper book 7) (2017)
126. The Final Act (The House of Jack the Ripper book 8) (2017)
127. Stephen (2017)
128. The Spider (2017)

AMY CROSS

129. The Mermaid's Revenge (2017)
130. The Girl Who Threw Rocks at the Devil (2018)
131. Friend From the Internet (2018)
132. Beautiful Familiar (2018)
133. One Night at a Soul Auction (2018)
134. 16 Frames of the Devil's Face (2018)
135. The Haunting of Caldgrave House (2018)
136. Like Stones on a Crow's Back (The Deal Trilogy book 2) (2018)
137. Room 9 and Other Stories (2018)
138. The Gravest Girl of All (Grave Girl book 3) (2018)
139. Return to Thaxos (Dead Souls book 13) (2018)
140. The Madness of Annie Radford (The Asylum Trilogy book 3) (2018)
141. The Haunting of Briarwych Church (Briarwych book 1) (2018)
142. I Just Want You To Be Happy (2018)
143. Day 100 (Mass Extinction Event book 6) (2018)
144. The Horror of Briarwych Church (Briarwych book 2) (2018)
145. The Ghost of Briarwych Church (Briarwych book 3) (2018)
146. Lights Out (2019)
147. Apocalypse (The Ward Z Series book 3) (2019)
148. Days 101 to 108 (Mass Extinction Event book 7) (2019)
149. The Haunting of Daniel Bayliss (2019)
150. The Purchase (2019)
151. Harper's Hotel Ghost Girl (Death Herself book 4) (2019)
152. The Haunting of Aldburn House (2019)
153. Days 109 to 116 (Mass Extinction Event book 8) (2019)
154. Bad News (2019)
155. The Wedding of Rachel Blaine (2019)
156. Dark Little Wonders and Other Stories (2019)
157. The Music Man (2019)
158. The Vampire Falls (Three Nights of the Vampire book 1) (2019)
159. The Other Ann (2019)
160. The Butcher's Husband and Other Stories (2019)
161. The Haunting of Lannister Hall (2019)
162. The Vampire Burns (Three Nights of the Vampire book 2) (2019)
163. Days 195 to 202 (Mass Extinction Event book 9) (2019)
164. Escape From Hotel Necro (2019)
165. The Vampire Rises (Three Nights of the Vampire book 3) (2019)
166. Ten Chimes to Midnight: A Collection of Ghost Stories (2019)
167. The Strangler's Daughter (2019)
168. The Beast on the Tracks (2019)
169. The Haunting of the King's Head (2019)
170. I Married a Serial Killer (2019)
171. Your Inhuman Heart (2020)
172. Days 203 to 210 (Mass Extinction Event book 10) (2020)

173. The Ghosts of David Brook (2020)
174. Days 349 to 356 (Mass Extinction Event book 11) (2020)
175. The Horror at Criven Farm (2020)
176. Mary (2020)
177. The Middlewych Experiment (Chaos Gear Annie book 1) (2020)
178. Days 357 to 364 (Mass Extinction Event book 12) (2020)
179. Day 365: The Final Day (Mass Extinction Event book 13) (2020)
180. The Haunting of Hathaway House (2020)
181. Don't Let the Devil Know Your Name (2020)
182. The Legend of Rinth (2020)
183. The Ghost of Old Coal House (2020)
184. The Root (2020)
185. I'm Not a Zombie (2020)
186. The Ghost of Annie Close (2020)
187. The Disappearance of Lonnie James (2020)
188. The Curse of the Langfords (2020)
189. The Haunting of Nelson Street (The Ghosts of Crowford 1) (2020)
190. Strange Little Horrors and Other Stories (2020)
191. The House Where She Died (2020)
192. The Revenge of the Mercy Belle (The Ghosts of Crowford 2) (2020)
193. The Ghost of Crowford School (The Ghosts of Crowford book 3) (2020)
194. The Haunting of Hardlocke House (2020)
195. The Cemetery Ghost (2020)
196. You Should Have Seen Her (2020)
197. The Portrait of Sister Elsa (The Ghosts of Crowford book 4) (2021)
198. The House on Fisher Street (2021)
199. The Haunting of the Crowford Hoy (The Ghosts of Crowford 5) (2021)
200. Trill (2021)
201. The Horror of the Crowford Empire (The Ghosts of Crowford 6) (2021)
202. Out There (The Ted Armitage Trilogy book 1) (2021)
203. The Nightmare of Crowford Hospital (The Ghosts of Crowford 7) (2021)
204. Twist Valley (The Ted Armitage Trilogy book 2) (2021)
205. The Great Beyond (The Ted Armitage Trilogy book 3) (2021)
206. The Haunting of Edward House (2021)
207. The Curse of the Crowford Grand (The Ghosts of Crowford 8) (2021)
208. How to Make a Ghost (2021)
209. The Ghosts of Crossley Manor (The Ghosts of Crowford 9) (2021)

AMY CROSS

For more information, visit:

www.blackwychbooks.com

AMY CROSS

Printed in Great Britain
by Amazon